The terrorist held Kuragin in a death grip, knife at her throat

Mack Bolan let up on the trigger. All he could see of his adversary was one foot and one ear. For a few seconds no one moved.

The Japanese shifted so that he could study the Executioner. "You are the man from last night. The one we were not able to kill. You will drop your pistol or the woman dies." He pressed the blade against the Russian's neck to emphasize his demand.

"Kill her," Bolan growled.

"You would stand there and let me slit her throat? You would let your own countryman die?"

"I'm not Russian. I'm American."

"Whatever you are, I do not believe you want her harmed. Drop your weapon and step back."

The woman's eyes pleaded with Bolan. "Do not worry about me. Shoot him!"

The terrorist cuffed the Russian behind her head. "Shut up!"

The Executioner saw his chance. The Japanese had unwittingly exposed half his face. But the numbers had run down.

From the stairs outside came the thud of running feet. Reinforcements had just arrived.

MACK BOLAN ®

The Executioner

DON PENDLETON'S
THE EXECUTIONER®
ROGUE AGENT

A GOLD EAGLE BOOK FROM
WORLDWIDE.

TORONTO • NEW YORK • LONDON
AMSTERDAM • PARIS • SYDNEY • HAMBURG
STOCKHOLM • ATHENS • TOKYO • MILAN
MADRID • WARSAW • BUDAPEST • AUCKLAND

First edition July 1995
ISBN 0-373-61199-4

Special thanks and acknowledgment to
David Robbins for his contribution to this work.

ROGUE AGENT

Revenge is a kind of wild justice, which the more man's nature runs to, the more ought law to weed it out.

—Francis Bacon,
1561-1626

It takes a cold, unfeeling heart to exact revenge when the price is measured in the number of innocent lives lost. We all have it in our nature. Let's hope we know when to say "enough."

—Mack Bolan

THE
MACK BOLAN®
LEGEND

Nothing less than a war could have fashioned the destiny of the man called Mack Bolan. Bolan earned the Executioner title in the jungle hell of Vietnam.

But this soldier also wore another name—Sergeant Mercy. He was so tagged because of the compassion he showed to wounded comrades-in-arms and Vietnamese civilians.

Mack Bolan's second tour of duty ended prematurely when he was given emergency leave to return home and bury his family, victims of the Mob. Then he declared a one-man war against the Mafia.

He confronted the Families head-on from coast to coast, and soon a hope of victory began to appear. But Bolan had broken society's every rule. That same society started gunning for this elusive warrior—to no avail.

So Bolan was offered amnesty to work within the system against terrorism. This time, as an employee of Uncle Sam, Bolan became Colonel John Phoenix. With a command center at Stony Man Farm in Virginia, he and his new allies—Able Team and Phoenix Force—waged relentless war on a new adversary: the KGB.

But when his one true love, April Rose, died at the hands of the Soviet terror machine, Bolan severed all ties with Establishment authority.

Now, after a lengthy lone-wolf struggle and much soul-searching, the Executioner has agreed to enter an "arm's-length" alliance with his government once more, reserving the right to pursue personal missions in his Everlasting War.

PROLOGUE

The jeep's bright headlights sliced through the crisp winter night and framed a guarded gate in their harsh glare. Mikhail Dorsakov saw the two sentries and promptly eased his foot off the gas pedal. He raised his head high enough to check on his fake mustache and beard in the rearview mirror, then quickly turned up the collar of his heavy coat so it partially hid his face.

Both young guards were inside a simple shack, huddled in front of a portable heater that rested on a small table. When the headlights bathed them, they grabbed their weapons and rushed outside. They had their subguns in hand and were looking properly official by the time the jeep crunched to a stop in the snow.

Dorsakov slowly rolled down his window. He saw one of the pair glance at the markings on his vehicle. The sentry stiffened, poked his companion, and they snapped to attention.

"We were not told to expect anyone tonight, sir," commented the senior of the pair.

Dorsakov handed over his forged papers. "Life is full of surprises, soldier. That is why those who seek to advance in rank know it is wise to always expect the unexpected."

"Yes, sir," the man responded. He made a perfunctory show of examining the ID and handed it back, as if afraid it would set his fingers on fire. "Sorry to have detained you, sir."

"Nonsense," Dorsakov said. "You are merely doing your job. Carry on." He touched his hat and waited for them to open the gate, then drove into the sprawling compound. At that time of night there were plenty of empty parking slots near the entrance. He grabbed his attaché case and hustled to the double doors.

One of the gate guards had to have phoned ahead because a burly sergeant stood there to greet him, opening the door and snapping to attention with a flourish. "May I be of service, sir?"

"No," Dorsakov replied. "I will be only a moment. I must drop off papers for Professor Konev." He realized he had made a mistake the moment he mentioned the nonexistent papers, but it was too late. Squaring his shoulders, he marched off before the sergeant presumed to question him.

Having studied the blueprints carefully, Dorsakov knew exactly where to find Konev's laboratory on the second floor. It was unlocked. The office at the rear proved to be another matter.

Dorsakov glanced over a shoulder, listened a minute, then quickly opened the attaché case and took out a vibrating pick. He inserted the thin tip into the lock and flicked the switch. In seconds the pick had shaken the tumblers into position, making no more noise than a quiet electric shaver in the process.

The door creaked open at Dorsakov's touch, and he swiftly crossed to the safe. Here subtlety was out of the question. Working with care, he applied a wafer-thin strip of plastic explosive around the edge of the safe door, attached a slender detonation cord and backed out into the lab with the small electronic detonator in one hand and the attaché case in the other.

Dorsakov set the case down between his legs and leaned against the wall to brace himself for the concussion to follow. He was taking a risk blowing the safe, but he had no other choice. His sources claimed the vials were kept in an unbreakable titanium-alloy case, and he hoped they were right.

"Please make no sudden moves, or I will be forced to shoot you."

Dorsakov slowly twisted his head. It was the sergeant, as he knew it would be.

"I kept asking myself why someone would be dropping off papers in the middle of the night when he could just as easily send them through proper channels," the sergeant said while advancing warily. "And now I see that—"

The detonator hit the floor with a smack. Dorsakov had deliberately let go. The instant the sergeant's eyes flicked down, Dorsakov's other hand swept up holding a Bernardelli 9 mm pistol. He stroked the trigger twice, and at each cough of the suppressor the sergeant jerked backward.

Eyes fluttering, the noncom oozed to the floor.

Dorsakov lost no time in setting off the explosive. He was on his feet before the sound of the blast died out. The safe door had been neatly separated from its housing. It was the work of a moment to grab the handle of his ticket to turn and to whirl and hasten out.

The young gate guards were shivering and stamping their feet in the below-zero cold when Dorsakov steered his jeep onto the road. He was in such fine spirits, he smiled and waved. Then the night swallowed him.

Four hours later the biggest manhunt in the history of Russia began.

1

The sleek Messerschmitt-Bolkow-Blohm BO 105 helicopter streaked in low over the mountainous terrain to avoid detection by radar. Mack Bolan, its sole passenger, gazed out the tinted canopy at the rugged gorges and sandstone uplands and thanked his lucky stars the German pilot was rated one of the best. The remote reaches of the Black Forest had claimed its fair share of unskilled pilots over the years.

"Two minutes, Herr Belasko," the captain said in clipped English.

"Thanks," Bolan replied. He did a final weapons check. Between the M-16, the Beretta 93-R, the .44 Desert Eagle and the various lethal tools of his trade he carried in utility belts, the big man believed he was as ready as he would ever be.

The only complaint Bolan had about his latest mission was the daylight insertion. He risked losing the element of surprise, which was critical when the odds against him were so high. It was wiser to penetrate a terrorist stronghold under cover of darkness, but in this instance he had been left with no choice.

Hal Brognola had made that clear. The director of the covert Sensitive Operations Group for the United States Department of Justice had told Bolan outright that there had never been a mission where timing was more crucial. "You have to get in there and take them out before they fly the coop, Striker," the big Fed had said. "Just spare one or two so we can get some answers."

Which was easier said than done, Bolan reflected. In a firefight there were no guarantees, and he had told the man as much.

"That I know. Just do your best."

Now, seconds from touchdown, the warrior hoped his best would be good enough. Many innocent lives were riding on the success of his mission. He held the M-16 in both hands and peered ahead for the clearing that would serve as his kickoff point.

Suddenly they were there. The pilot swooped in swift and low and set the BO 105 down as delicately as if on thin ice. He gave Bolan the thumbs-up sign as the warrior went out the door. Pausing just a moment to get his bearings, the big man bent low and sprinted into the trees, the prop wash buffeting his camouflage fatigues.

Like a dragonfly arcing into the sky, the chopper swept up and away and was lost from sight in moments.

The Executioner consulted his compass. The compound was supposed to be due northeast of his position. If he proceeded on an azimuth of sixty degrees, he should eventually reach a ridge overlooking it.

The warrior tucked the compass into a pouch and broke into a dogtrot he could maintain for hours. A thick forest of dark fir and spruce surrounded him, quiet except for the chirping of birds. Underfoot a carpet of pine needles muffled the tread of his combat boots.

All went well until Bolan unexpectedly came on a narrow gorge that shouldn't have been there. Crouching, he pulled out a packet containing the aerial photo map Brognola had been supplied by German intelligence. He double-checked the grid coordinates and frowned. He was right on track. It was the map that was at fault. The grid where the gorge should be contained nothing but trees.

Bolan had no idea how the mistake had been made. It mattered little whether human error, computer error or another factor was to blame. He had a job to do. Folding the map, he stepped to the edge of the precipice and weighed his next step.

The gorge was less than twenty feet wide but five times as deep. The sides were steep, too steep for anything but a mountain goat to negotiate without proper equipment.

Turning to the left, the warrior hiked a hundred yards in the hope the gorge would end and he could go around. Unfortunately he had no such luck. Since he couldn't afford to waste any more time, Bolan searched for a likely spot to descend and found a cleft that reached from the rim to the bottom.

Without delay the warrior slung the M-16 over his shoulder, knelt and eased onto his stomach. He glanced at the bottom, deciding a course of action. Exercising delicate care, he slid his legs over the brink and shimmied lower until his elbows hooked the rim.

Bolan bunched his stomach muscles, took a breath and lunged backward, jamming his back against one side of the cleft and his hands and feet against the other. He dug in his heels and waited a few moments, breathing deeply to prepare himself for the exertion to follow.

By moving first one leg and then the other and bracing himself with his rigid spine, the big man slowly descended. Rough spikes of rock poked his flesh. It was agonizing work. Bolan's calf muscles and thighs ached horribly before he reached the bottom. He was grateful when he set foot on solid ground again and took a minute to stretch the kinks and cramps out of his legs.

Scaling the other side proved just as difficult. Bolan used whatever handholds were available, sometimes clinging to the smooth stone surface like a human fly. He was caked with sweat when he finally clawed his way over the rough rim and moved into the shadow of a pine to catch his breath.

Bolan wasn't one to believe in omens, but he had to admit that so far the mission was off to a less-than-auspicious start. He could only hope the map was correct in all other respects, that the missing gorge had been a fluke.

It wasn't. The warrior covered more than a mile and had yet to find the ridge. Once again he checked the map and once again discovered the grid layout was wrong. His intuition blared a warning in his mind. There might be more to the foul-up than seemed apparent, he mused. If that was the case, then instead of springing a surprise assault on a pack of terrorists, he could be walking into a trap.

Bolan slung the M-16 a second time and climbed a tall fir. Perched on a high limb, he spied a low mountain to the east from which a spine extended in his direction. It wasn't the ridge, but it was the next best thing.

Keenly aware of the time factor, the big man set off at a brisk clip. When the trees thinned at the base of the spine, he slowed, using whatever cover was at hand. Clusters of boulders enabled him to gain the summit without exposing himself. Once there, he crouched in the shadow of a monolith and raised a pair of pocket-size binoculars to his eyes.

A pristine stream gave them away. Bolan reasoned their lair would be near water, so he followed its winding course with the binoculars, up onto the bottom slope of the adjacent mountain. There he spied several log structures well hidden in the pines on the left bank.

"Got you," Bolan said to himself. He backed off the crest and circled around to come up on the stream from the south. Alert for hidden cameras and other security devices, he paralleled the stream until he drew within three hundreds yards of the compound.

The warrior climbed another tree for a bird's eye view of the layout. A shack stood nearest the facing slope of the mountain. To its left was a long, low structure that might serve as a bunkhouse or warehouse. The house itself sported three stories with balconies on the second and third. There was no fence, probably a concession to give the place the appearance of a typical mountain lodge. Nor were there any guards. No movement was evident even though he scanned the stronghold a dozen times.

Bolan had been told that years ago the retreat had been a hideaway for a wealthy German fond of the outdoors. Game was abundant, fish were plentiful and there were scores of sheer peaks to climb in the summer and steep slopes to ski in the winter. Somewhere along the line October Dawn, as the terrorists styled themselves, had come into possession of the place. How, no one knew.

Descending, the warrior worked his way in a wide loop that brought him up on the stronghold from the rear. He had yet to spot anyone moving around, which bothered him. German Intel assessed October Dawn as having nine members. The latest report, which had been

in Brognola's hands all of five minutes when the big Fed
dispatched Bolan, claimed all nine were at the lodge.

Like a living shadow, the Executioner flitted from
tree to tree and boulder to boulder until he was within
a stone's throw of the shack. Power lines ran from a
pole beside it to the other buildings, which alerted Bolan to the fact the shack housed a generator. Since no
telltale hum disturbed the quiet, he knew the generator
was off. Further confirmation that no one was home.

Bolan snaked to the shack and rose with his back to
the rear wall. He crouched at the corner to study the
house. A door was visible, but so were tinted windows
on each of the three floors. A terrorist might spot him
and Bolan would never know it. He glanced at the sun,
which hung hours above the horizon, then thought of
the urgency involved.

The warrior sprinted for the door, executing a weaving pattern to minimize the target he presented. He let
his combat boot do the knocking. The door splintered
under the impact, and he found himself in a spacious
kitchen. Neatly stacked dishes stood on a counter. No
one was present, and there was no evidence anyone had
been there in a long time.

Bolan dashed to the next doorway, which opened
onto a narrow hall. The M-16 tucked tight to his shoulder, he ran down the middle, swinging right and left as
he came to other doors, none of which were closed. He
passed bedrooms, bathrooms and a small storeroom.
There were no signs that anyone had lived in any of the
rooms for quite some time.

At the end of the hall a flight of spiral wooden stairs
led to the second floor. Bolan took them three at a
stride, bending low near the top and elevating his head
by gradual degrees until he felt confident no one waited

to ambush him. Veering to the right, he backed against a wall and listened. Nothing.

In front of Bolan the corridor widened into a gallery of sorts that overlooked an enormous living room. He could see the cold hearth, an empty sofa, a number of plush chairs covered with sheets of clear plastic to keep off dust.

The warrior began to think that the terrorists had indeed flown the coop. Before venturing to the third floor he checked all the rooms along the hall and found them deserted. In the last room he stepped out onto the balcony to survey the grounds. Still nothing moved. The lodge was like a graveyard.

Bolan returned to the spiral stairs. He took the same precautions, which again proved unnecessary. There were fewer rooms, but they were all just as vacant. He checked in closets, in drawers, but found no clothes.

Brognola would be ticked off, Bolan reflected. The big Fed had counted on having the answers they needed before the day was out, and now they had to start over from scratch.

The big man descended to the living room. He checked the ashtrays, verifying they were empty and clean. Next he stepped to the fireplace and touched the charred bits of wood to make certain they weren't warm. At last he had to face the undeniable truth.

Bolan slung the M-16 over his right shoulder and walked to a tinted window. There was no telephone or he would simply call Brognola. Instead he had to wait for the chopper to return in an hour. Sixty more minutes would be wasted, and the world would be that much closer to a nightmare of devastating proportions. He decided to make a thorough search of the entire premises on the off chance he'd find a clue to the band's destination.

Bolan started in a room on the ground floor that gave every appearance of having been the terrorists' answer to a tactical center. Bookshelves lined the walls, except one wall that had been plastered with maps of Europe, England and the United States. In the center, two desks had been placed back to back, and at the rear sat a long, low table ringed by folding chairs.

The warrior examined the maps first. Dozens of tiny holes told him where pins had been stuck. Most were major cities on the Continent, a few in small towns and others in rural areas. Taking a small pad and pen from one of his pockets, Bolan made a list of the sites. While they meant nothing to him, the Stony Man operations team might be able to piece together important Intel.

The desks attracted Bolan next. He went through both from top to bottom, drawer by drawer. All were empty. He rapped on the panels, hoping to find a hidden compartment, but there was none.

He turned his attention to the bookshelves. They contained the usual radical mishmash of books devoted to leftist propaganda, global doom and gloom, and an entire shelf of pornographic material. In one corner he came across several government manuals. He knew a little German and was able to tell they were from the defense ministry and had been stamped Confidential.

Bolan started to carry the manuals to the desks. Brognola would be interested in learning that October Dawn was able to obtain classified German documents with apparent ease. He happened to glance down and spotted a folded sheet of paper under the nearest desk. Setting the manuals down, he sank to one knee and retrieved the paper. As he rose, he unfolded it. There were two paragraphs in scrawled German.

Suddenly the short hairs at his nape prickled. His combat-honed senses had registered a whisper of air where there shouldn't be any. He let go of the sheet and whirled, bringing the M-16 to bear as he did. But as fast as he was, he wasn't quite fast enough. A portion of one of the walls had swung silently out to reveal a secret room and a tall blond man in an expensive suit who held an oversize pistol. The moment Bolan set eyes on him, the man fired.

2

Even as the man in the suit squeezed the trigger, Mack Bolan realized that the big pistol was actually a small grenade launcher. In the blink of an eye the grenade struck him, hitting him squarely in the chest as he began to squeeze off a burst. For a frozen instant the warrior thought he would be blown to bits. Then the impact lifted him off his feet and smashed him onto the desk, while simultaneously being enveloped in a thick cloud of yellowish-green gas.

The launcher had fired a tear-gas canister, not an explosive shell. Bolan tried to hold his breath, but it was too late. The choking fumes invaded his nostrils and seeped down his throat. He scrambled to escape the cloud, but only went a few feet when his insides twisted into a terrible knot and his head threatened to burst. Whatever type of tear gas had been used was remarkably potent. He sagged, too weak to move, helpless for one of the few times in his life.

A pair of vague figures materialized beside him. Bolan tried to draw the Beretta, but his hand was kicked aside and both pistols were snatched from their holsters. Rough hands hauled him to his feet, and he was propelled out of the study and along the hall to the living room where he was dumped on the floor. He tried to keep from coughing and wheezing but couldn't.

Out of the corner of one eye, Bolan saw the blond man who had fired the tear gas now removing a gas mask. The grenade launcher was in plain sight, a 40 mm Heckler & Koch Model 69 A-1 that weighed under five pounds and could fit in a fair-size pocket. The man tossed it on the sofa, pulled back the flap of his jacket and pulled a Glock 17.

Bolan heard another man speak rapidly in German. The tall blonde answered, and hands frisked him from head to toe, plucking weapons as they went. He was flipped onto his back and saw a stocky black-haired man in rugged alpine clothes glaring down at him.

"You must be wondering why you are still alive, my American friend," the blonde said in heavily accented English. "Tell me your name and I will tell you."

The warrior tried to speak, but his throat felt as if it had been scraped raw with sandpaper. He took deep breaths and rubbed his eyes.

"I am waiting."

Bolan struggled onto his elbows while making a show of trying to speak. His gaze roved the lodge, confirming the two hardmen were its only occupants. He looked out the windows but saw just the trees. Then he made up the first name that came into his head. "Forrest," he croaked. "My name is Forrest."

"Well, Mr. Forrest," the man said, and paused. "Or should I call you *Agent* Forrest, since you are no doubt a very special operative of the United States government?" The suave shooter took a seat on the sofa, the Glock pointed at the warrior's head. "You are alive because we require certain information. You will stay alive only as long as you continue to cooperate. Understood?"

Bolan merely nodded. His lungs still burned as if they were on fire, and his nose and eyes were running but he had regained enough of his strength to sit up. He saw the stocky man holding an Uzi on him.

"My name is Joseph, and my friend there is Franz," the blonde said. "I work for the German government in a capacity that need not concern you. I also assist October Dawn on occasion." He leaned down and plucked the photo maps from the pile of Bolan's hardware and gear. "I trust that you had a hard time finding the lodge? I altered these in the hope you would not find it at all, but you must be a very persistent man."

The statement explained a lot. Bolan put two and two together and said, "Let me guess. The terrorists pay you for your services. You're a German Fed who is on the take."

"What quaint expressions you Americans think up." Joseph grinned. "And how astute of you. It takes a lot of money to support me in the style to which I have become accustomed, as you would say."

"And October Dawn has robbed a lot of banks," Bolan said. He'd met the man's kind before, traitors to their country, betrayers of those who hired them. Men and women who put greed before honor, who worshiped money before all else. "How did you hook up with them?"

Joseph made a clucking sound. "*Nein, Herr Forrest.* I am the one who will ask the questions." He tossed the map to the floor, leaned back and let the Glock rest on his lap. "Now, you will tell me everything your government knows about October Dawn and why you were sent to eliminate them."

"Do you have all day?"

"I warn you," Joseph said. "I have no time to bandy words. If you do not provide the information, I will have Franz shoot your legs off at the knees and slowly work his way up your body until your tongue loosens."

There was no doubt Franz would do what he was told. Bolan remembered the face from the mug shots Brognola had shown him. Franz Bitner was a member of the terrorist group and had a long history of prior arrests.

"This is what I do know," Joseph stated. "Our branch of the defense ministry received a special request from your government for all the information we had on October Dawn. About the same time, some of our men got lucky and located this hideaway. My superior contacted your people, who arranged to have you flown in." He paused. "You will fill in the gaps, starting with the reason the U.S. government is so interested in October Dawn all of a sudden."

Bolan noted a feral glint in Franz's eyes. All it would take was a nod from Joseph, and the terrorist would cut loose. Since the warrior had no desire to die needlessly, and since revealing the truth wouldn't compromise any sensitive classified information, he said, "Novichok-5."

"I thought so."

The warrior knew that the word had spread like wildfire through the intelligence community weeks earlier. A rogue Russian had stolen one of the most lethal chemical agents ever created, Novichok-5, and every government was on the lookout for the man. His capture had become the highest priority of Interpol, Scotland Yard and La Sûreté Nationale, to name just a few.

"So your people know about the auction, do they?" Joseph stated. "I told Berta that she was being foolish if she thought it could be kept a secret."

The auction the German referred to was being set up by the rogue Russian, who intended to sell the Novichok-5 to the highest bidder. Berta Stein, Bolan had learned from Brognola, was the brutal leader of October Dawn, a fanatic who once gunned down several unsuspecting police officers for the sheer pleasure of it.

Joseph trained the Glock on Bolan again, then spoke rapidly to Franz in their native tongue. The terrorist grunted and walked off. "You have been most helpful, Herr Forrest. I have learned all I need to know."

"Oh?"

"I am not stupid, American. Now we will dispose of you in the manner Berta requested, and I can be on my way."

Bolan tensed. He wasn't about to go meekly to the slaughter. He had to be ready to take advantage of the first opportunity that presented itself. If one didn't, he'd have to take the initiative.

Joseph apparently liked to hear himself talk. "You have no idea how much trouble you have put me to. I took a great risk tampering with the information we relayed to your people, but I needed to buy as much time as I could. The only way for me to warn Berta was to come all the way out here in person."

At the rear of the lodge a door slammed. Bolan deduced that Franz had gone outside. Why, he had no idea, but he was sure it didn't bode well for him.

"Unfortunately I could not sneak away from Bonn until about three hours ago. It would have been so much easier to use a shortwave, but I dared not risk having the frequency monitored."

"Your government will nail you eventually," Bolan said. "Traitors always give themselves away in time."

The German agent reddened with anger. "Insult me as you will, Herr Forrest. In a very short while I will spit on your corpse. And I think you will agree it is better to be a live traitor than a dead patriot."

The Executioner took a gamble in an attempt to provoke the dirty Fed into doing something stupid. "I bet your mother and father are proud of how you've turned out. They should be overjoyed when they read about you in the papers."

It was a childish insult no professional would give a second thought, but Joseph bristled and rose, extending the Glock. Just when the warrior thought the traitor would pull the trigger, Joseph calmed himself and shook his head. "No. This would be too easy. And Berta is paying me good money to do it her way." He walked to the right, giving Bolan a wide berth. "It would have been better for you if you had not found the lodge, Herr Forrest. To be candid, I was hoping you wouldn't. No matter what you think of me, I do not relish killing a fellow agent."

Bolan was disappointed that Joseph hadn't come a little closer. He had no weapons other than his hands and feet, but they were all he needed.

"I can't wait to have this done with so I can get out of here," Joseph rambled on. "It was Berta's idea that Franz and I stay to give you a suitable reception. I would have refused if not for the extra money she is paying me." He chuckled. "In a few hours I will be sitting at one of the best restaurants in Munich dining on Wiener schnitzel and fine wine. Berta and I will drink to your health."

Every muscle in Bolan's body was keyed to make a leap, but the German stayed out of reach. It was obvious that the man was nervous, perhaps afraid that others would show up before he could clear out. The warrior decided to use that to his advantage. "Berta Stein will have to drink alone. I didn't come here by myself. In a little while this place will be swarming with agents."

"I know better," Joseph replied, refusing to take the bait. "My superior was quite clear on the fact your government was only sending in one operative. We talked about it at length, wondering what sort of man you must be. Now I can see that you are not so special."

Bolan took the insult in stride. The door at the back of the lodge slammed again and Franz reappeared, holding a long length of coiled rope.

"You may stand now," Joseph said, adopting a two-handed grip on the pistol. "You will follow Franz, holding your hands above your head. And it goes without saying that you will make no sudden moves, unless, of course, you care to die that much sooner."

The warrior complied, falling into step behind the terrorist, who headed for the spiral staircase and climbed to the second floor.

"You will appreciate the trouble we are going to on your behalf, Herr Forrest," Joseph said sarcastically. "Berta has a fine flair for the dramatic."

Bolan made no reply as they walked to the gallery overlooking the living room. Franz stepped to the small railing and began to uncoil the rope. Joseph moved wide to the left so he would have a clear shot at the Executioner, and leaned back against the rail.

"Are there any more quaint phrases you would care to say at this time?" the turncoat taunted.

Ignoring the man, Bolan watched Franz, who kept glancing at the nearest of six overhead beams. Each one was two feet in diameter and about the same distance from the ceiling. The terrorist swung one end of the rope and hurled it at the beam but missed by inches. He tried again with the same result.

Joseph impatiently tapped his foot. He jabbed a finger at the beam while snapping instructions in German.

Franz didn't seem pleased. Reluctantly he unslung the Uzi and tied the end of the rope to the sling. Then, facing the beam, he planted his feet firmly and swung the weapon in a tight circle. When he let go, the rope flew up and out, but the angle was off and the Uzi clattered against the beam instead of sailing over it. Franz cursed while reeling the rope in.

It wasn't hard for Bolan to guess their intent. He kept glancing at Joseph, hoping the man would let down his guard for just a second, but he had no such luck.

Franz, muttering, tried again. By sheer fluke the machine pistol arced up and over the beam, its momentum swinging it back into the terrorist's hands. He untied the Uzi and slung it over his shoulder. Next he made a noose in the rope, tied the other end to the railing and turned toward the warrior.

"The moment of truth, Herr Forrest," Joseph said smugly. "Are you a movie buff?" he asked, and went on before Bolan could answer. "I was as a child. American Westerns were always my favorites. I must have seen dozens of hangings, but never one in real life." He paused. "Until now. You will be so good as to step to the rail."

With the muzzle of the Glock fixed on him like an unblinking eye, Bolan had no choice but to do as he was told. The terrorist jerked his arms down, then stepped behind him and slipped the noose over his neck. The rope felt rough, like twine. The thick knot was wedged under his chin.

Joseph sidled closer. "I wonder how many seconds it will take to strangle the life from your body?" he mused. "This should be most interesting." He moved closer, reached into a jacket pocket, produced a set of handcuffs and wagged them at Franz.

Bolan knew that once they slapped the cuffs on him, he was as good as dead. If he was going to act it had to be right then. With the thought came action. He suddenly reached up and gripped the thick rope with both hands even as he vaulted onto the rail and launched himself into space. So unexpected was his move that Joseph stood there, frozen in amazement. Franz made a grab for him but missed.

It was an insane gamble born of desperation. Bolan shot outward, whipping his legs as would a gymnast. There was little slack and no jolt as the rope took his full weight. His bulging arms and shoulders bore the brunt of the strain, but there was still enough pressure on his neck to give him the sensation of having a fist mashed into his throat. At the apex of his swing he spun and whipped his legs forward a second time, which sent him hurtling toward the gallery.

Joseph and Franz had stepped right up to the rail. They were so astounded by the unforeseen turn of events that neither had thought to bring a weapon to bear. On seeing the man in black swoop toward them, they finally reacted. Franz tried to bring the Uzi into play, while Joseph whipped up the Glock and snapped off two shots. Both missed by a hair.

Then Bolan slammed into them. His legs as rigid as steel, he plowed into them with the force of a battering ram. Franz was struck in the face and went flying into the far wall. Joseph took the Executioner's other foot in the chest, the jarring impact flinging him toward the stairs. The Glock went spinning away.

The warrior had mere seconds to free himself. His momentum started to carry him back out over the living room. He knew if that happened, he would die, either from being unable to keep the noose from tightening or from a hail of lead. With a deft twist he hooked a leg around the upper rail, while tugging with all his might on the slip knot. It refused to budge.

Bolan saw Franz start to rise, shaking his head to clear it. Again he yanked and tore at the knot. This time it loosened, not much but enough for him to wrench the noose over his head. He jumped to the floor, took three swift strides and reached the terrorist just as Franz grabbed for the Uzi.

The warrior delivered a front snap kick to his adversary's face. The ball of his foot caught Franz squarely on the nose. Blood spurted as the terrorist was hurled back into the wall. He was dazed but still game and assumed a boxing stance to defend himself. Bolan moved in close, ducked under a jab, then drove a spear hand thrust into the terrorist's ribs. Franz collapsed like a deflated balloon.

Although the Executioner knew better than to take his eyes off an enemy in a close combat situation while the enemy was still alive, he did just that, pivoting to confront Joseph—only the traitor wasn't anywhere in sight.

Without warning, Franz struck, his leg flicking out and catching the warrior behind the knees. Bolan was upended but rolled to the right and regained his feet in one fluid motion. As he did, Franz lunged, a gleaming knife in his right hand. The razor tip came close to slicing open Bolan's right eye. He backpedaled, evading thrust after thrust. Suddenly Franz smiled. Bolan had no idea why until he took his next step backward and bumped into the railing. He had gone as far as he could go.

Instantly Franz closed in.

3

Mack Bolan shifted as the knife speared past his face. He swept both hands up and grabbed the terrorist's wrist. Then, twisting and bending at the waist, he flipped Franz Bitner over his shoulder.

The hardman uttered a shriek of rage as he went over the railing. He flailed the empty air, clawing for purchase that wasn't there. When he hit there was a loud thud and a sharp crack. Franz went limp, his lifeless eyes fixed on the very beam from which he had planned to hang the Executioner.

The warrior whirled and scooped up the Uzi. He darted to the spiral stairs but saw no sign of Joseph above or below. Bolan started down, then paused. Ten feet away, half hidden by a hall door, was the Glock. He realized it had to have been knocked from Joseph's hand when he kicked him, but it still didn't explain why the terrorist had fled.

Bolan bounded down the stairs. At the bottom he scanned the living room, tempted to reclaim his gear but knowing he couldn't afford to take the time. The Uzi tucked to his side, the warrior headed down the hall toward the kitchen but drew up short when he glanced back and saw the front door was open. It had been closed earlier.

Reversing direction, Bolan dashed to the door and crouched against the jamb to scour the area beyond. A rutted dirt track that served as the road to the outside world meandered off to the southeast. Going around a bend several hundred feet away was the renegade German Fed.

The warrior pushed off in pursuit. In the fleeting glimpse he had of Joseph, it was obvious the man had been badly hurt. That kick in the chest, Bolan reflected, had to have caved in a few ribs. He poured on the speed. Instead of sticking to the road, he angled into the woods.

Through the trees Bolan saw the German doubled over, with a hand pressed to one side. He also saw a motorcycle hidden in high weeds adjoining the road. Joseph was almost to it when the Executioner burst from the pines a few yards behind him and leveled the Uzi. Under different circumstances Bolan would have shot the man without a second thought. But Brognola wanted someone to interrogate, and Joseph just might have the information the Justice man needed.

"That's far enough!" Bolan commanded.

Joseph stopped and turned, his face a mask of agony.

"You're going back with me. A friend of mine has some questions he'd like to ask you."

"I should have shot you instead of listening to Berta," Joseph said bitterly. "Now it is all over. My days of fine living are at an end."

"At last we agree on something." Bolan motioned with the Uzi. "Move it. I don't have all day."

The agent straightened with a visible effort. "You do not understand, Herr Forrest. If I cannot get away, then I am going nowhere."

"You don't have any choice in the matter," Bolan reminded him. "Since you're so fond of American sayings, here's another. I hold all the aces."

"Except one," Joseph said somberly. Spinning, he darted to the motorcycle, a small dirt bike.

"Forget it," the Executioner growled, surprised the man would be so foolish. "You're not going anywhere." He took a step to the right and saw that Joseph wasn't trying to climb on the bike. A pannier case was attached to the back of the cycle, and the German agent was opening it. His hand plunged inside and reappeared holding a stainless-steel Ruger P-85. The click of the safety being worked was loud in the crisp mountain air.

Bolan no longer had any choice. He triggered the Uzi before Joseph completed a turn. The slugs ripped into the agent's side, punching him back against the dirt bike. The man was dead on his feet but somehow managed to raise the Ruger, so the Executioner fired another burst. The slugs drilled into the traitor and he fell, toppling the cycle as he went down.

The warrior strode forward to verify the kill. Some of the rounds had punctured the dirt bike, rendering it unusable. He consulted his watch, then headed for the lodge. The minutes were ticking down, and he still had a job to do.

HOURS LATER Bolan walked along a street not far from Stachus Square in Munich. He wore a trench coat, his head covered by a cap, his hands in his pockets. Under his left arm rode the Beretta, under his right the Desert Eagle.

Ahead, The Gustav House boasted delicious food and drink. Bolan paused in an archway under the sign and slapped the cap against his coat. To an observer it would seem he was removing excess water. Actually he was checking to see if he had been followed or if anyone loitered in the vicinity. It was no on both counts.

Replacing the cap, the warrior strolled inside. Brognola's contact in German intelligence had seen to it that a reservation had been made under the name of Mike Belasko, but Bolan still had to wait to be seated. As he was being led across the dining room he pointed to a table at the rear and the waiter obliged. Bolan sat in a chair against the wall and accepted a proffered menu. Over the top of it he surveyed the room.

The restaurant was packed, and more than twenty women were present. Bolan figured that Berta Stein would be by herself but none of those he saw were seated alone, none fit the description of the murderous radical. Were it not for the fact the German authorities had established that Joseph Amberg made reservations for eight o'clock, Bolan would have doubted he was at the right place.

When the waiter returned, the Executioner ordered the Wiener schnitzel and sat back to study the women. The older ones he mentally chalked off right away. The same with two young girls. Berta Stein, he recalled, was in her middle twenties, so he concentrated on those who appeared to be about that age.

A few minutes later Bolan found his quarry. She wore a blond wig but there was no mistaking her face or the large mole on the side of her neck. Two men were at her table. One Bolan recognized as Helmut Dortmund, another member of October Dawn. The third man was unknown to him.

Bolan willed himself to relax so he could enjoy his meal. For an hour or so, at least, he could pretend to be a typical American tourist. After that he had to take one of those terrorists alive and not harm any innocent German civilians in the bargain.

He ate lightly in order not to be sluggish when the time came. Berta Stein, he noticed, often glanced at her watch and at the entrance. Joseph's absence would bother her. She would be doubly wary when she left, and the Executioner had to be equally so if he was to take her by surprise.

Eventually Dortmund asked for the check, and the trio walked to the register to pay.

Bolan beckoned for the waiter and handed him twenty more deutsche marks than the bill called for. "Pay it for me and keep the change," he said, standing and sauntering toward the entrance of the restaurant as Berta and her friends went out the door.

"*Danke,*" the waiter called after him.

Donning the cap, Bolan peered out the door before pushing on it and saw that Stein and her cronies had turned to the right. He waited until they were out of sight, then emerged and trailed them, hugging the shadows. They had linked arms and behaved as would carefree college students, talking loudly and laughing. At the next corner they took a left.

Bolan picked up the pace. He halted shy of the corner and cautiously looked around it. The threesome were halfway up the block.

Several taxis drove by, but Stein didn't hail one. For ten minutes the trio moved steadily eastward, from the business district into an industrial sector where huge foundries lined narrow streets.

Fewer and fewer pedestrians passed by, and streetlights became few and far between. It suited Bolan perfectly. He reached under his jacket to loosen the Beretta, confident his chance would soon come. Up ahead, the trio turned yet another corner.

As usual, Bolan stopped and looked. The sight of Stein and the men running like the wind caught him off guard. He thought that they hadn't detected his presence.

Breaking into a sprint, the warrior sped into the open. He stopped abruptly when he realized there were only two fleeing figures, Stein and Dortmund. At the same split second he spied a glint of metal in a doorway on the left and threw himself to the pavement. He heard the cough of a suppressor, and a slug bit into the ground close to his ear. The warrior unleathered the Beretta and responded in kind.

The chug of Bolan's automatic was greeted by a loud grunt. The man in the doorway staggered into the street, his arms dangling at his sides, and buckled.

The Executioner was in motion before the man hit the ground. He had lost sight of Stein and Dortmund, and for a few moments thought they had eluded him. Then he spotted the pair going into a building on the other side of the street. He veered across and down to an alley that flanked the building, an old foundry that appeared to no longer be in use.

The warrior cut into the alley and crept to a broken window. Inside, footsteps crunched and someone whispered. He sprinted to the far end. Crouching, he catfooted to a rickety loading dock, then up to the back door. Someone had already paid the place a visit. The window in the top half of the door had been broken, and the door stood wide open.

Bolan went in fast and low, scooted to the right and froze with his back to the wall. It was pitch black. Gradually his eyes adjusted enough for him to make out dim shapes. Off to the right a few dozen yards, something clattered to the floor. One of the terrorists was being careless. Or had it been deliberate?

Staying low, the warrior moved in the direction of the sound. He placed each foot carefully, the soft soles of his boots hardly brushing the floor. A wide, squat silhouette rose before him, and it took only a second for him to identity it as a flight of concrete steps.

A scuffing sound came from the second floor. Bolan didn't know whom the terrorists thought they were kidding, but it wasn't him. They were luring him higher, undoubtedly into a trap. Maybe they knew the area and had hidden in the foundry previously. Of course, knowing he was walking into a trap didn't stop him from doing so. The lives at stake outweighed the risk.

Bolan eased up the right side of the steps, his body hugging the wall. A breeze struck his face as he neared the top, and from the next step he saw why. There was a gaping, jagged hole in the foundry roof. Pale starlight bathed the middle of the huge floor.

The Executioner dropped flat and crawled up the last step. Alert for the slightest noise, he kept going toward the wall. Plenty of debris and refuse littered the floor, forcing him to detour. He was almost there when a mouse scampered out from under a box in front of him and squeaked off into the gloom.

Bolan heard a distinct footstep to his rear. He shoved upright and ran in a weaving pattern as behind him the foundry rocked to the blast of submachine-gun fire. A mini-Uzi, Bolan guessed. Leaden hornets buzzed all around him or spanged off the floor and wall. He took a running dive and wound up behind a pile of discarded wooden crates.

Suddenly the clip in the subgun ran dry. In the silence that ensued, someone retreated into the darkness.

The warrior recalled that Berta Stein had carried a big purse. He rose and used the crates for cover as he moved forward a half-dozen yards.

Going prone again, Bolan crawled until he could see the stairs. There was no movement in that direction, which told him the terrorists were determined to see him dead. Maybe they wanted revenge. Stein was smart enough to put two and two together and might suspect he was the same man who had been sent to the lodge. Given her bloodthirsty nature, she'd want his head.

Bolan slid to the right, staying wide of the pale patch of starlight. His combat-honed instincts told him the terrorists were doing the same. It was just a matter of time before they made a mistake, or he did. And it didn't have to be a big mistake, either. The scrape of a knee, the scuff of a toe, was all it would take.

At the limits of the warrior's vision a shadow detached itself from the surrounding darkness and moved from left to right, toward the wall. Turning, Bolan crawled back the way he had come. Only instead of going to the wall, he went around the end of the crates and rose to his knees on the other side.

Keeping an eye on the corner, Bolan waited, as motionless as the wooden crates he was pressed against. He heard the stalker before the person was close enough to see, heard the soft scrape of stealthy steps. Whoever it was paused often. Then a figure appeared, pistol held at waist level.

It was Helmut Dortmund.

Bolan could have cored the terrorist's brain with ease. But he had yet to take one alive. Here was another chance, and he had no intention of blowing it. He coiled to surge from hiding but changed his mind when Dortmund unexpectedly walked toward the crates. The Executioner thought he would have to shoot but the terrorist moved toward the other side and passed from sight.

The warrior immediately crept around the stack. He was mere yards from Dortmund's back. A few more steps was all it would take, and he could knock his prey unconscious.

As if sensing the warrior's presence, Dortmund whirled and brought up his autopistol. His reflexes were almost equal to the occasion; he got off one shot before Bolan reached him.

The Executioner chopped the hard edge of his left hand into the terrorist's wrist, batting the autopistol down at the moment it went off. The bullet drilled into the floor. Without missing a beat, Bolan drove his elbow into Dortmund's face. The terrorist staggered against the crates, blood spurting from his nose, and gamely tried to lift his pistol.

Bolan whipped around, driving a backhand into the side of the terrorist's head. Groaning, eyelids fluttering, Dortmund pitched onto his side.

The patter of running feet filled the chamber. The warrior looked up and saw Berta Stein bearing down on him. She didn't believe in a stealthy approach. Screaming her rage, she cut loose with her mini-Uzi.

A line of holes stitched across the crates, zeroing in on Bolan. He hurled himself onto his belly with a heartbeat to spare. The slugs ripped into the wood inches above his prone form, then started to track back toward him. The warrior raised the Beretta and stroked the trigger twice, and Berta Stein went down.

Bolan rose slowly. The mission had taken a lot longer than he had counted on, but he had Brognola's package, and October Dawn had lost their leader. He headed toward Stein to confirm she was dead but stopped when Dortmund groaned again and moved. Bolan walked over and picked up the man's pistol, a 9 mm Mauser Luger.

Dortmund was tougher than most. The average man would have been out for an hour or more. Not Dortmund. He sat bolt upright, his hands seeking the pistol that wasn't there.

"On your feet," Bolan ordered, pointing the Beretta at the man's gut. *"Hinauf!"*

Dortmund wore a scowl as he rose. "American pig!" he growled. "You think you are so clever, tracking us here. But we—"

Bolan saw the man glance past him and grin. It could only mean one thing, though the testimony of his own eyes told him that was impossible. It also meant he was dead unless he moved, and moved fast.

The mini-Uzi opened up as the warrior darted to the left. He saw Dortmund's sly grin transformed into a grisly grimace as the Parabellum hailstorm meant for Bolan tore into the terrorist's chest. The German was slammed into the crates and took several with him as he fell.

Executing a long, rolling dive, Bolan pushed to his feet near the end of the stack and leapt behind them in time to beat the next burst. He caught a glimpse of Stein on her feet, her face twisted by hatred. Then he had the crates behind him and was making for a mound of debris twenty feet away. Once there, he ducked and waited for the woman to show herself.

Usually when Bolan shot someone through the heart, that person dropped dead and stayed dead. There had to be a reason for Berta Stein's miraculous recovery, and Bolan guessed the miracle was called Kevlar. Her dress had been on the baggy side. Now he knew why.

A minute dragged by, but Stein didn't reappear. The warrior knew she was up to something, but he was at a loss to pin down her purpose. As more minutes elapsed and no sounds broke the deathly stillness of the abandoned foundry, he decided to go on the offensive. He was at a disadvantage, though, because she was the last one alive and he had to take her down without taking her out, a job on a par with declawing a leopard that hadn't been tranquilized.

Bolan rose high enough to see above the debris. He was so intent on the stretch of floor in front of him that he almost missed the whisper of movement to his rear. Spinning, he saw a slender shape flit down the steps. Stein had circled around him and was trying to escape. Or so he assumed.

The big man jogged toward the landing. He was almost there when Stein began shouting angrily in German, the stream of words too swift for him to follow. Outside the building, a vehicle door slammed.

Premonition carried Bolan on winged feet to the nearest window. The pane was smeared thick with dust, but he could still see the brown van parked at the curb. Several men had already spilled from it. As Bolan gazed down three more slid from the passenger side, then closed a sliding door. There were six, all told, and every one was armed.

A second later the murderous pack of political assassins entered the foundry.

4

The members of October Dawn were fanatical leftists who felt that everyone else should think as they did. Those who didn't were fair game.

The German government blamed October Dawn for dozens of deaths and suspected them of many more. Bombings, kidnappings, drive-by shootings, October Dawn had done it all and added a few flourishes of their own. For instance, they liked to kill in exotic ways. A judge had met his end in a hot tub after an electric heater was thrown in with him. A banker had been smeared with pig fat and tossed into a pit of ravenous dogs. And a member of the Bundestag, the German parliament, had been lashed to a long pole and barbecued over flaming charcoal.

In short, October Dawn was as vile a bunch of self-righteous cutthroats as Bolan had ever run up against. They were part and parcel of the forces of evil the warrior had dedicated his life to opposing. Where most men would have feared for their lives, the Executioner felt a renewal of his sense of purpose.

Bolan backed from the window and jogged to the landing. The terrorists would want to finish him off quickly, before someone heard the gunfire and thought to notify the police. It would make them rash, and in a firefight being rash was as sure a way to die as committing suicide.

Sure enough, two men appeared at the bottom of the steps and charged upward. In the dim light it was hard for Bolan to tell, but he was able to make out that one of the pair held a G-3, a German army service rifle with full-auto capability. The other held a Sten Mark II subgun.

The big man braced himself on one knee and extended both the Beretta and the Mauser Luger he had taken from Dortmund. He let the two terrorists get halfway up, then he put a slug between the shoulder blades of each.

The warrior had to throw himself backward as several terrorists brought their weapons into play. Lunging to his feet during a break in the action, he skirted the steps and ran along the left-hand wall toward the rear. It proved fortunate he did, because he was barely out of range when a grenade went off with a powerful roar, blowing a hole in the steps and swirling dust high into the air.

Bolan found another flight of stairs down, but as he put a foot on the first one, excited whispers warned him that the terrorists had already cut him off. He hit the floor barely in time. A submachine gun and a shotgun chewed the step to bits and would have done the same to him had he been a shade slower.

The warrior was boxed in. He couldn't go down, yet the enemy gunners, if they wanted, could sneak onto his level since he couldn't cover both stairs at once. Eventually they would nail him if he sat there and did nothing. He jogged to the nearest window to see how close the next building was to the foundry. It being too far, he went to the next. And the next.

At the fourth window, on the side of the foundry, Bolan hit pay dirt. It overlooked the roof of a large structure. The best news was that the two buildings were separated by a mere eight feet.

He cocked his head and listened for the terrorists. For a reason he couldn't fathom, they were still below. He wondered if they had explosives and were hoping to blow him up.

Bolan faced the window. Using the Mauser, he smashed out the pane, breaking any jagged shards that would cut him. Harsh yells broke out, and boots drummed on the steps. The warrior backed up a good twenty feet, wedged both pistols under his belt, then sprinted toward the window.

The cool night air hit the big man in the face as he leapt from the foundry and dropped toward the roof of the other building. Eight feet wasn't far, but it was far enough that the jolt of landing would have sent pain lancing up his legs and spine had he not held himself loose and rolled on impact. As he came to his feet he saw a terrorist framed in a window on the lower floor. The man had a shotgun and took a step back to raise it to his shoulder. The step proved costly.

Bolan drew the Mauser Luger and fired from the hip, emptying the clip, puncturing window and terrorist both. The window dissolved in hundreds of shards. The terrorist melted from sight, the shotgun slipping from his lifeless hands and tumbling over the sill.

The warrior didn't stay to watch the gun hit. It was only a matter of seconds before the rest of October Dawn caught on to his ruse and dashed to the same side of the foundry to pick him off. He tossed the Luger aside and raced toward the front of the smaller building, seeking a way inside. To the right was the block outline of an air conditioner. Farther along he came to a door and tried the knob. It was locked.

He could hear Stein shouting orders to her troops in the foundry. One of the windows exploded, revealing two terrorists with subguns.

In a flash Bolan had the Desert Eagle out. He fired twice into the door and drew back his right foot to kick as the roof was bombarded with autofire. The door shattered under the first blow. The warrior went down a short flight of stairs and took cover around a corner until the gunners stopped chewing up the exit.

He climbed swiftly to the doorway. Both terrorists were still framed in the window, in the act of reloading. Neither paid any attention to the roof. They were amateurs, Bolan reflected, elevating the Desert Eagle. One shot apiece was all it took. For the moment all the windows on that side were clear of terrorists. Bolan turned to go back down the stairs but thought better of the idea when he spied the top of a fire escape at the southwest corner.

Covering the foundry as he ran, the warrior reached the corner and looked down. The unattended van was less than thirty feet from the bottom of the fire escape. Bolan descended rapidly, leaping down the flights of metal steps. At the last one he stopped, temporarily stymied because the ladder to the ground had been pulled up. He knew it would waste precious seconds if he took the time to lower it, so he went over the side and dropped to the pavement.

A short sprint took the Executioner to the van. He ran behind it and stood so he could see the front of the foundry through the windows.

Sirens wailed in the distance.

Bolan knew that Stein and her companion wouldn't remain inside much longer. Half a minute later they barreled out the front door. Casting repeated glances at the other building, they raced to the van. The warrior bent at the waist and ran around the front of the vehicle. He came to the end of the front fender at the same instant that the male terrorist started around. The man never knew what hit him. Bolan slammed the Desert Eagle into his forehead, and as the man collapsed he aimed at Berta Stein, who was reaching for the door handle. "Your choice," he said.

The scourge of Germany showed her mettle and tried to bring her Uzi into play.

Bolan's finger caressed the trigger once. The big .44 boomed and bucked. Berta Stein, nailed in the shoulder, was smashed into the door. She lost her grip on the machine pistol and slumped to the ground. She made a grab for the Uzi, but Bolan was there ahead of her and slammed his foot on her wrist.

"Damned American!" Stein rasped, spitting on his shoe.

The warrior picked up the mini-Uzi and stepped back. "Tell me about the auction, Stein."

"Nein!" she grated. "Never!"

"That's what you think."

THE PRIVATE JET SOARED through the sky like a great gray bird of prey. Mack Bolan opened his eyes and stared at the matchbox-size farms and villages below. The nap had done him good. Stretching, he glanced over his shoulder at the rear section, which had been partitioned off from the rest of the aircraft so the pair of black-suited interrogators could work in private. Once, before dozing off, Bolan had heard a wail of baffled fury, no doubt when Berta Stein had been injected with the thiopental sodium or whatever pentothal derivative the psych-probe boys were using of late.

The partition door opened and out walked Hal Brognola. The big Fed looked the worse for wear. His eyes had bags under them from lack of sleep, and his suit had that crumpled, slept-in appearance. He sank into the seat across from the warrior with a long sigh. "We finally got it all out of her, Striker, though you wouldn't believe the fight she put up. Even under the drugs, she fought us. I've seldom seen a will so strong."

"What about her accomplice?"

"Leipzig knew nothing. He was the newest recruit to October Dawn, and I doubt Stein fully trusted him yet." Brognola wearily rubbed his eyes.

"This one is getting to you, isn't it?" Bolan asked.

"Is it that obvious?" Brognola replied, running a hand over the stubble on his chin. "Yeah, I guess it is. Can you blame me? Novichok-5 is the single most lethal biochemical warfare agent ever created. If it's unleashed in a major urban area, the death toll will be in the hundreds of thousands. And if whoever is high bidder can get their hands on the technology needed to manufacture more on their own, we're talking millions of lives."

"So where is the auction to be held?"

Brognola shifted in his seat. "Near the Pyrenees Mountains."

"The French side or the Spanish side?"

"In France," Brognola said. "Not far from the Garonnes River." He paused. "There's a remote château once used as a safehouse by the KGB whenever they needed to hide some of their boys from our boys. The Château d'Ours it was called in the old days."

"KGB," Bolan said. "That fits. Mikhail Dorsakov was a KGB agent for seventeen years."

"One of their very best. He was their top specialist at monitoring terrorist activities worldwide. So he knew all the right people to contact about his auction." Brognola pulled a sheet of paper from a pocket and began to unfold it. "As much as I hate to admit it, this idea of his is positively brilliant. Just imagine. Inviting the heads of some of the most powerful terrorist organizations from around the globe to bid on the weapon of their dreams. It's diabolical."

"Do we have any idea exactly how many have been invited to attend?"

"No," Brognola answered, and tapped the sheet. "But we have a fair idea. Thanks to Stein, I can up the number to seven bidders." He ticked them off. "The Red Dragons from Japan, the Popular Liberation Front from Turkey, the Burning Light from Chile, an unidentified group from Ireland but presumably the IRA, a Somali warlord, of all things, and two other organizations. We believe one will come from Italy, the other from Cyprus."

"How do you want this handled?"

"In and out," Brognola said. "I toyed with the idea of having you infiltrate the meeting as the representative from October Dawn, but the invitations are for the heads of each group."

"No one else can go?"

"Each is allowed a single companion. Our friend Dorsakov isn't taking any chances."

"He's playing with fire," Bolan said. "The people he has invited won't hesitate to kill him to get their hands on the Novichok-5 without paying a cent if they think they can get away with it."

"I'm sure Dorsakov knows that." Brognola became somber. "As much as we want him terminated and the heads of the various organizations disposed of, it's the Novichok-5 we want the most. Once you're in there, if things go wrong, try to bring out the vials even if you accomplish nothing else."

"Understood. Do we have a layout of the château?"

"We will after we touch down at Marseilles. Everything we need will be waiting for us, including your papers and a Jeep."

"A Jeep?"

"The château is so remote there isn't an airport within a hundred miles. It would be risky dropping you in. And, too, if you need to get out in a hurry, it would be better if you had your own transportation to rely on."

"Are we working with the French on this one?"

"Yes and no. We've told them that we've traced the rogue Russian into their country, but we haven't given them the location yet. They'd insist on sending in a special ops unit and we don't want that. Dorsakov might be killed before he turns over the Novichok-5."

"What if Dorsakov doesn't have it at the château?"

"There is that possibility. He might have hidden it somewhere, and the highest bidder will be told the location. But it's a chance we have to take. Which brings me to a request I have to make."

"Don't tell me. Let me guess," Bolan said. "You want me to take Dorsakov alive if at all possible."

"Only if you determine the Novichok-5 isn't at the château," Brognola responded, frowning. "I know I'm asking a lot. You can't be one hundred percent effective when you have to hold back. But believe me when I say I hate it as much as you do, and if there was any other option I'd tell you to do what had to be done. Only this time we don't have a choice.''

"I know," Bolan said. He disliked having to go into a firefight with one arm tied behind his back, as it were, but he could see the big Fed's point. "The Novichok-5 has to come first."

"I have one other request."

"What is it now?"

"Make it out alive."

BOLAN NEVER FAILED to appreciate the long reach of Brognola's influence. In his capacity as director of the Sensitive Operations Group for the United States Department of Justice, it sometimes seemed as if the big Fed had contacts in every country on the globe and in half the cities. No matter where they might be, whatever Brognola wanted—even on short notice—was delivered where and when it should be.

Marseilles was no different. The jet coasted to a stop in front of a small hangar at one end of the bustling airport. Parked inside was the Jeep, crammed with all the gear Bolan would need. Its fuel tank had been topped off. Bolan placed the duffel bag containing his hardware, fatigues and blacksuit in the back seat. A man in a gray suit gave Brognola a package that he examined briefly, then handed to the Executioner. It contained maps and as much information as was known about the Château d'Ours.

Brognola stood beside the vehicle as Bolan slid in behind the wheel. "You're on your own from here on out," the big Fed commented, his worry lines deepening. He pointed at the passenger seat. "Your radio is hidden under there, set to the frequency we'll be monitoring. Once you have the Novichok-5 and need to be extracted, get on the horn. I'll have a chopper there as fast as I can."

Bolan gripped the keys in the ignition.

"One other thing," Brognola said. "There's a gas mask in the black pack in back, but I wouldn't rely on it if I were you. Intel indicates the biochemical agent doesn't have to be inhaled to be lethal. It can be absorbed right through the skin. Through the clothes, in fact. So if one of the vials is broken, your best bet is to get upwind as quickly as possible."

Brognola gazed out the hangar at the city, then went on. "Did you know that the prevailing winds at this time of year could carry the biochemical from the château to here in about three hours? And since Novichok-5 is colorless and odorless, the first we would know about it would be when people started dropping like flies." He shook his head. "The Russians outdid themselves with this one."

"Makes you wonder, doesn't it?"

"How's that?"

"If there are any more nasty surprises hidden away at other Russian research facilities, just waiting for someone like Dorsakov to come along."

"Thanks. You've just made my day."

The Jeep turned over smoothly. Bolan shifted into first, nodded at Brognola, and wheeled out of the hangar. He followed the road around the perimeter of the airport to the main gate, then headed due west.

Marseilles was packed with cars and pedestrians, as well it should since it was the second largest city in France and the country's leading seaport. To the south Bolan could see the Old Harbor. On a high hill, visible for many miles, stood the Notre Dame Cathedral.

Eventually the traffic thinned. The warrior passed the outskirts of Marseilles and followed the highway to Montpellier where he swung to the southwest around the Gulf of Lyons until he came to Narbonne. From there he struck off across rolling hills toward the distant Pyrenees.

The road narrowed. After a few hours Bolan seldom encountered other vehicles. The region was sparsely populated, with few villages and no towns. By late afternoon high peaks crowned the horizon as far as the eye could see. He pressed on until twilight shrouded the countryside, then pulled off the road into a grove of hundred-year-old beeches. By his best reckoning he was within an hour's drive of the château, but it would soon be dark and he couldn't very well study the lay of the land at night.

From among the supplies Brognola had provided, Bolan took a sleeping bag and spread it out beside the Jeep. He made a small fire and opened a can of beef stew, which sufficed as his supper. Afterward he turned in even though it was early. The next day promised to be a busy one.

Chirping sparrows woke the big man up when a band of pink lighted the eastern sky. He made coffee, polished off two cups and was on the road by the time the blazing sun appeared. His course took him over a ridge and down into a wide, beautiful valley where women wearing quaint red hoods tilled the fields. Situated beside a swiftly flowing stream was a small village known as Orthez. It was less than twenty miles from the château.

Bolan applied the brakes as he neared a stone bridge. A young woman who carried a walking stick was herding a dozen cows across the road, and he had to give them the right of way. She smiled coyly at him as she went past.

According to the Intel Brognola provided, the people of the region were reputed to be friendly but liked to mind their own business. That suited Bolan just fine, since the last thing he needed was inquisitive locals.

The sight of an open-air café reminded Bolan that he hadn't eaten any breakfast. He pulled over and took a table well back from the street. Three other tables were occupied. He pegged the customers as locals, none of whom paid any attention to him.

A dark-haired beauty in a colorful dress bustled out of the café. Balancing a large tray of food in one hand, she carried it to another table, then turned to go back inside. Her eyes settled on the warrior, and she did a double take. She approached him, but she had the nervous look of a frightened fawn ready to bolt. *"Bonjour, monsieur."*

"Good morning," Bolan said, smiling warmly.

The woman brightened and said in heavily accented English, "Ah. You are English, *oui?*"

"Close enough."

"Well, if you are not, you must be an American," the beauty declared, visibly relaxing. "And at least I speak your language, so I will not have any trouble like I did with those Orientals."

The comment caught Bolan's interest. Two of the terrorist delegates expected to attend the auction were from Japan, members of the Red Dragons. "Were they Japanese?" he asked casually.

"I honestly do not know," the woman said. "They did not speak French or English, and they were unbearably rude. One of them became so mad when I could not understand him that he gripped my wrist so hard it hurt."

"Tourists," Bolan said, and shrugged.

The woman laughed. "How true. And we have had more than our share in the past few days. Between them and the Parisians, there has been no end of excitement."

"Parisians?" Bolan asked, prompting the woman to provide more information.

As if on cue, a flashy yellow sports car squealed around a corner and screeched to a stop at the curb. Out climbed three toughs who strutted toward the tables as if they owned the place.

The woman's fright was plain to see. "Here they come," she whispered in warning, "and I am afraid they will cause trouble for you."

5

Mack Bolan folded his hands on top of the table. The trio in leather jackets had focused on him to the exclusion of all else. Like a pack of wolves slowly closing in on their quarry, they spread out as they approached him. The waitress squared her shoulders and faced them defiantly. She addressed them in her own language, the string of words too swift for Bolan to follow.

The tallest of the toughs halted in front of her. He had cruel, leonine features topped by a shock of sandy hair. The look he gave Bolan was one of utter contempt. "So," he said in English. "Monique tells me that you are an American. Perhaps you would be so good as to tell me your name and why you are in Orthez?"

The warrior made no reply.

"You would do well to answer me, stranger," the tall one said belligerently, and started to walk around the waitress.

Monique put a hand on his chest. "Enough, Jules!" she declared. "I have told you before about giving our customers a hard time. You will leave, at once."

"It is a public place, *non?*" Jules responded, pushing the woman's arm aside. He shouldered past her, leaned on the edge of the table and glared at the warrior. "I will not ask a third time. Who are you? Why are you here?"

Bolan looked the man right in the eyes. "What the hell is it to you?" he demanded.

Jules flushed scarlet and glanced at his companions. Both of them moved closer. "You are not very polite, American," he said coldly. "I think I do not like you very much."

"Then we're even," Bolan replied. He motioned at Monique with his head and gestured for her to get out of the way, but she simply stared at him, shocked that someone would talk to Jules in that manner. "Why don't you run along before someone tells your mother that you snuck out of the house again without her permission."

The tall Frenchman lunged toward Bolan, trying to grab hold of the warrior's jacket. But as fast as Jules was, he was no match for the Executioner. Bolan clamped a hand on the man's wrist, twisted and pulled. Jules yelped as he was slammed face-first into the table.

A burly hardman rushed to his companion's aid. Bolan merely shifted in his chair and drove his right foot into the man's knee. This one went down abruptly onto his back, clutching his leg and groaning.

The third guy came in swinging, two wild blows that Bolan easily ducked under. Not even bothering to stand, the warrior flicked a pair of swift jabs into the man's ribs and the ruffian slumped, his arms clasped to his chest. A follow-up blow sent him sprawling.

All three Parisians were on the ground. To Bolan's surprise, several of the patrons clapped their hands and smiled at him. Monique walked up to Jules, who was in the act of rising, and jabbed him with her toe.

"You will leave now, Jules Martel, and you will never bother anyone here again."

Blood trickling from his mouth, Jules stood. Pure hatred blazed in the look he gave Bolan. Then he helped his companions to rise. They shuffled to the sports car and sped off, burning rubber as they swerved around the Jeep.

Monique turned to Bolan. "You were magnificent, *monsieur*," she gushed. "At last someone stood up to those scoundrels." She caught herself and smiled. "No, you did not stand up, did you? You never left your seat."

"Why do you let them bully you?" Bolan asked. "Isn't there a police station in Orthez?"

"We are a small village, as you can see," Monique said. "We do not have *gendarmes* posted here."

Bolan leaned back. How convenient, he mused, for Mikhail Dorsakov. It had to have been another factor that influenced the rogue agent to pick the old château for the meeting. "Maybe someone should go to the nearest station and report Jules and his buddies."

"I have thought of doing so," Monique said, "but the man who owns the café is afraid they would cause him even more trouble if I did. So he has asked me to be patient. The Parisians are leaving in a few days, we were told. And since they stay at the château at night, it is not as if they are a constant nuisance."

"Is there a château close by?" Bolan played the innocent.

"The Château d'Ours," Monique said. "The castle of the bear, I think it would be in English." She pointed westward. "It is in the next valley. Very out of the way. Tourists never go there."

"Who owns it?"

"No one really knows. It was sold some years ago to a foreign buyer, or so the rumor went. No one has lived there regularly since, although every now and then someone will spend a few weeks or even months. Last month a man arrived and has stayed on. I do not know his name.''

''When did Jules and his friends show up?''

''About ten days ago. The man at the castle left for a short while, and when he returned they were with him. Frankly I do not see why he brought them. Jules told me once that they were hired to protect the château.'' Monique snorted. ''How silly. Protect it from whom? He was lying, I think, to impress me.''

Another customer caught her eye and she hurried off, leaving Bolan alone with his thoughts. He had learned a lot in those two minutes of casual conversation. It was Brognola's belief the auction was slated to take place within the next two days. The arrival of the Red Dragons confirmed it.

In a short while Monique returned to his table. ''My goodness. In all the excitement I forgot to take your order.''

Bolan ordered a continental breakfast with soft-boiled eggs. He tarried over his coffee, hoping the waitress would find another minute to spare. He wasn't disappointed. She strolled over wearing the friendliest of smiles.

''Would you care for anything else?''

''A little conversation would be nice,'' Bolan said. ''I've been on the road for a long time with no one to talk to.''

Monique glanced around the café, then abruptly sank into the chair across from him. ''And why not? I have worked hard all morning. Pierre will not begrudge me a short break.''

"You have me curious about the château," the warrior stated. He had to pick his words carefully in order not to make her suspicious of his motive. "Photography is a hobby of mine, and I'd very much like to photograph it."

"You would be wise to forget the idea," Monique advised. "Jules and his friends keep close watch on the road, and the man who lives there has made it plain he does not like uninvited visitors."

"How did he do that?"

"Some of the villagers took him a basket of cheese and wine when he first arrived, as a token of goodwill. He refused to accept their gift and told them not to step foot on his property again."

"Nice man," Bolan said. "I bet he's not French."

"*Non.* No one knows his nationality. In his way he is quite mysterious, as were those Orientals and the two black men."

"Black men?" Bolan repeated, thinking of the Somali warlord.

"Yesterday morning. One was an old, skinny man who carried himself as if he were a general. The other was built like a bull."

"Did they speak English?"

"The older man did. The bull did not utter a syllable the whole time they were eating."

"Any other strangers been by lately?"

"None that stopped. A limousine went past the day before last. I heard from a farmer that it took the cutoff to the château." Monique regarded him closely. "Where are you bound, if I might ask? Spain?"

"It's as good a place as any," Bolan hedged.

"Why don't you spend a day or two in Orthez? There are many fine sights for you to photograph, and you would have the pleasure of my company if you want it."

The proposition caught Bolan off guard. He had forgotten how forward Frenchwomen could be. His first thought was to tell her no. Then it occurred to him that it might suit his purpose better if he played the part of a typical tourist. It would divert any suspicions Dorsakov might harbor if the Russian learned of his presence. "Is there a hotel?"

"No, but Mrs. Delacroix has a room she rents whenever she can find a renter. Are you interested, monsieur..."

"Belasko. Mike Belasko. Yes, I am," Bolan admitted.

She gave him instructions. He paid and drove straight to the Delacroix residence, a modest house with a small courtyard. The elderly matron, who spoke a little English, was delighted to have him take the room. He paid for two days but made it plain to her that he didn't know how much time he would actually spend there.

THE HIGHWAY out of the village led due south, into the heart of the Pyrenees. Bolan kept alert for the cutoff, a dirt road that according to the map wound over a ridge into the next valley. As it was, he almost missed the turn. Flanked by tall trees, it was so well hidden that he was abreast of the road before he spotted it. He punched the brakes, threw the Jeep into reverse, then drove westward toward the summit of the ridge.

The warrior hadn't gone far when he spied a patch of metallic yellow bordering the road, up at the crest. He promptly applied the brakes again and climbed out, raising his binoculars. Under high magnifications he saw the sports car clearly. Jules and his two friends were seated on a log, smoking. If they were supposed to be guarding the approach to the château, they were doing a poor job.

To Bolan, they were nothing more than a nuisance, but a big one. He couldn't try to barge or to bluff his way past them, not when they probably had a radio and would inform their employer. No, he had to find a way around. Returning to the Jeep, he drove back to the main highway and headed south. Half a mile later he came to a densely wooded tract and drove the vehicle as deep into the pines as he could.

Bolan laid the duffel on the grass and opened it. He changed into camouflage fatigues, then strapped on military webbing that would hold the many special tools of his trade he needed to take along. He wore the Beretta in a shoulder holster under his left arm, the Desert Eagle on his right hip. He also took the M-16, with enough spare magazines to wipe out a small army. A backpack containing a few extras was the last item he needed for the probe.

The Executioner broke into a dogtrot that could eat up miles without tiring him. It took a while for his lungs to adjust to the rarefied air at that altitude, but within ten minutes he was running as smoothly as a well-oiled machine.

The pines screened him clear to the summit. From a small clearing he enjoyed a bird's-eye view of the next valley and spotted the imposing château right away. Like a great stone spider it sat on the east bank of a river. Ribbons of woodland radiated from near its walls like the green strands of a gigantic web.

Bolan descended the gradual slope toward one of those ribbons. To his left towered a stark, barren mountain more than nine thousand feet high. Off to the right he occasionally glimpsed the road, the sports car still parked beside it.

Once on the valley floor the warrior picked his way forward with caution. He had no idea how elaborate a security system Dorsakov had set up, but he had no doubts there was one. The Russian wouldn't be foolish enough to rely only on Martel's bunch.

It took the better part of the afternoon for Bolan to get close enough to suit him. From a weed-choked knoll he could see most of the grounds. He lay prone, then took up the binoculars, which were tinted to reduce glare.

Five vehicles were parked in a circular drive. One was the limo Monique had mentioned.

The high, circular towers and steep roof of the Gothic-style structure reared several stories into the air. There were dozens of windows and a half-dozen doors. A separate conical tower, half as high as the château, stood a score of yards from the east wall.

Neither the driveway nor the buildings interested Bolan at that particular moment. He was intently studying the grounds surrounding the château, annoyed that once again the Intel Brognola had obtained was faulty.

No one had mentioned a maze.

Enclosing the château on all four sides was an enormous maze that showed evidence of long neglect, but was still intact. It was at least thirty yards wide. There were only two openings that Bolan could see. He tried to find a way through the bewildering network of thickets, but couldn't. Without a map to guide him, it might take hours to reach the château.

Suddenly a man appeared at an upper window. Bolan trained the binoculars on him and recognized one of the Red Dragons. The man held a drink and was smiling. Apparently Dorsakov knew how to keep his guests entertained.

The sun dipped to the horizon and melted from the heavens. As stars sprinkled the firmament, Bolan took a Starlite scope from his backpack, which he mounted to the M-16. It was a second-generation model of the type he had used extensively in Vietnam. As soon as he bent his eye to the eyepiece, he discovered the security system.

Dorsakov had gone to the trouble and expense to install an infrared perimeter defense grid. No doubt fitted with a special IR filter that made the laser beams invisible to the naked eye, it canvassed the ten-yard strip of grass between the maze and the château.

The warrior wasn't pleased. Getting in and out quickly would now be out of the question unless he discovered a weak link in the chain of defenses the wily rogue had set up.

Search as he might, the Executioner found none he could exploit. The driveway ended short of the maze. Bolan guessed that Dorsakov had met each of the delegates outside it and escorted them to the château, which was clever. If any of the terrorists tried to double-cross the Russian, they would have a difficult time escaping.

The more Bolan learned, the more convinced he became that he was up against one of the most skilled operatives he had ever encountered. As the old cliché went, the man didn't miss a trick—which made Bolan wonder if there were more security defenses inside the château.

He lowered the Starlite scope and slid down the back of the knoll. He had learned all he could for the moment. His best bet was to return to the village and track down the one item that might enable him to beat the maze. He could only hope that Brognola had been right about the date the auction was being held. If not, if it was sooner, they were dead in the water.

The warrior retraced his steps to the Jeep. He stowed the items he had taken, changed clothes and headed for Orthez. By now it was too dark for him to see the sports car. He checked the rearview mirror from time to time for headlights but none appeared.

Orthez was quiet as only a small country village could be at that early hour of the night. He parked and walked across the courtyard toward a door on the side of the house. Suddenly someone appeared in the shadows. Automatically Bolan reached for the Beretta but stopped when the person moved into the light.

"You are a lucky man, Monsieur Belasko," Monique said. "I was just about ready to go home. Now you can treat me to a drink and enjoy my sparkling conversation."

Bolan had to grin despite himself. "Then I must be the lucky one. Is there a tavern in town?"

As it turned out, the café doubled as the local watering hole after dark. It was crowded with townsmen and farmers. Monique found them a corner table. For the next hour they made small talk with her doing most of the talking. Bolan knew she liked him and had to admit that he found her equally attractive. But he knew he couldn't afford the luxury of an intimate interlude. He might be under surveillance by those he had come to eliminate, which would put his companion at risk.

Monique was unable to hide her disappointment when Bolan suggested he drive her home. She declined, saying she would like to stay and talk to some friends. Her eyes followed him to the door. He waved, but she didn't wave back.

ONCE AGAIN Bolan pulled up in front of the courtyard. As he opened the door of his vehicle and stepped out, three shapes detached themselves from the shadows.

Jules Martel and his two friends walked forward, holding switchblades. Martel grinned and wagged his knife at Bolan. "Did you think we would forget about you, bastard?" he hissed. "All day we have been waiting for this chance, and now we will pay you back for the insult of this morning."

Bolan wasn't about to waste breath arguing. Already they were so close that if he tried to go for the Beretta they would be on him before he could draw. For that reason he decided to take them down using the hand-to-hand combat techniques he had honed to a razor edge. He might have chanced going for a gun, but the noise would bring the matron and her neighbors on the run. They would insist on sending for the police, who would insist on interrogating him, forcing him to put in a call to Brognola so the big Fed could pull a few strings. It would blow his cover and, worse, might prevent him from putting his plan into effect.

The three men fanned out. It was plain they had done this before and knew how to work in concert to kill their victims with a minimum of fuss.

Bolan read their intent easily. They would come at him in a rush, all three at once, knowing he couldn't protect himself from so many adversaries at the same time. An average person couldn't, anyway. But Bolan was far from average.

At a barked word from Jules Martel, the men sprang forward, their knives extended to slash and cut, aiming high, at the big man's chest.

Bolan went low, dropping into a crouch and spinning into a leg sweep, his right foot slamming into the ankles of two of the toughs and upending them. Martel coiled and thrust, his switchblade spearing at Bolan's throat. The warrior twisted aside, gripped Martel's arm and spun, hurling the man into another attacker as the man tried to rise.

The third Parisian was also rising. Bolan slid in close, blocked a blow at his face and drove his elbow into his adversary's throat, crushing it. The tough gurgled and sputtered, but not for long. Stepping behind him, Bolan looped an arm around the man's neck, looped his other over the guy's head and wrenched sharply. There was a loud crack, and the Frenchman went as limp as a wet towel.

The other two attackers had regained their feet. Enraged, Martel snarled and leapt. Bolan shoved the dead man into him and they both went down in a jumble of limbs.

The other man had grown prudently wary. He came in with his knife at waist level and flicked it at Bolan in short strokes.

The warrior backed up, dodging each stroke, until he came to a tree. He glanced over the tough's shoulder and saw Martel untangling himself. He had to dispose of this one quickly so he could give his undivided attention to Martel.

Bolan tried to lure his adversary closer. He held out his left arm, hoping the man would take the bait and swing, but this one was too crafty. The warrior darted to the right. The man went after him, swinging at his leg. Throwing himself forward, the Executioner seized the tough's arm and whipped it in an arc. The man did a somersault and fell heavily onto his back, stunned. Before the thug could stand, Bolan tore the switchblade from his grasp, and sank the blade to the hilt in the man's chest.

Behind Bolan there was a strangled cry of outrage. He whirled and got his arms up barely in time to defend himself. Jules Martel, wielding two switchblades now instead of one, tore into him like a berserk whirlwind.

6

It had been Mack Bolan's experience that men who didn't care if they lived or died made the deadliest enemies. They took risks no levelheaded professional would ever take. In this instance Martel had been driven into a rabid rage by the deaths of his friends, and he wanted Bolan dead no matter what it took. So he rushed the warrior with the two knifes flashing, seeking to overwhelm him by the sheer force of his attack.

But Bolan wasn't easily overwhelmed. He kept his wits about him as he retreated before the crazed attack. When Martel stabbed both knives at him at once, the Executioner threw himself to the left, onto his shoulder, even as his right hand plunged under his jacket.

Martel, thinking Bolan had tripped, grinned in triumph and stepped in to finish him off. Martel drew up short when the muzzle of the Beretta was suddenly thrust in his face. The suppressor chugged twice, and it was over.

Bolan glanced at the house. The lights were on, but no one looked out or came to the door. He walked to the street and looked both ways. No pedestrians were in sight. He had been lucky. Now he had to work swiftly before the bodies were discovered.

First the big man dragged them into the shadows at the base of the wall enclosing the courtyard. Then he rummaged in Martel's pants pockets for a set of car keys. A short walk around the block turned up the yellow sports car parked between two buildings where it wouldn't be readily spotted. He drove it to the Delacroix house and loaded in the three corpses.

Bolan kept the car to a crawl until he was out of town. Then he buried the gas pedal. Half a mile from the outskirts he spotted a vehicle coming toward him. He switched off his headlights, veered off the highway, crossed a ditch and sped into a field grown high with wheat. He continued on fifty feet, then braked and turned off the engine.

A minute or so later the other vehicle drove past, a flatbed truck piled high with small pines. The driver never gazed at the field.

Only after it had disappeared from sight did Bolan fire up the car and circle around to the road. A mile farther on he reached dense woodland. Slowing, he sought an opening in the trees, and on finding one he drove into the gap. Limbs battered the doors and roof; brush clawed at the bumpers. The suspension shook and shimmied from the rough terrain. He traveled several hundred feet, winding ever deeper among the trees, stopping when a wall of closely spaced spruce barred his path.

Bolan checked the glove compartment but found nothing of interest. He turned to the bodies and went through the pockets he hadn't searched earlier. In Martel's leather jacket he found a key that interested him. It was old, ancient even, and made of iron. It was just the sort of key that might open a door to a building that had been around since the Middle Ages, such as the château.

Each of the Frenchmen had a wallet thick with francs. Money from Dorsakov, no doubt. He relieved them of their riches and their driver's licenses and other papers. Using a rag he found in the trunk, he wiped the car clean of his prints.

Bolan climbed out, then broke off low limbs and tore up brush, enough to cover the car from end to end. It was so well camouflaged when he was done that no one would spot it unless they were right on it. The licenses and IDs he buried in a small hole. The money he kept. It might come in handy sometime during the mission.

It was a long walk back to Orthez, but Bolan didn't mind. It gave him time to think. He had half a mind to take the Jeep and go camp somewhere in the woods until morning. The only thing that stopped him was the possibility of kindly old Mrs. Delacroix coming to harm because of him. If the rogue Russian knew he was staying at her place, Dorsakov might send other hardmen there. And if he was gone, they might torture her in the belief she would know where to find him.

It all depended on whether Martel had told Dorsakov about the clash at the café. Bolan's gut instinct was that the man hadn't. Martel wouldn't want his employer to know the three of them had been defeated in a fight by a supposed tourist. So maybe Mrs. Delacroix wasn't in any peril, but to be on the safe side Bolan decided to stay the night. In the morning he would go and not return.

Bolan was almost to the village when the growl of a high-powered engine made him turn. A big car rapidly approached. He ran down a short embankment and hugged the grass at the bottom. The headlights played over the top of the bank but went nowhere near him.

After the car had passed, he climbed to the highway in time to see the vehicle clearly.

It was the black limousine from the château.

The warrior jogged on once the limo was out of sight. He turned one corner, then another. Ahead was an intersection just north of the café. When he got there he spotted the limo parked in front of it.

Bolan drew back from sight. A few minutes later the door opened and out strode a tall man in a gray suit, his stern, hawkish features exactly as they looked in the photos Brognola had obtained of Mikhail Dorsakov. The former KGB operative was flanked by the two Red Dragons members and another man. They huddled by the limo awhile, scanned the street, then climbed in and slowly cruised off in the opposite direction.

Now what was that all about? the warrior wondered. He had to know, so as soon as their taillights disappeared around a bend, he hurried to the café.

The crowd had thinned. Farmers were famous for being early to bed and early to rise, and rustic villagers weren't much different. He saw no sign of Monique, which was just as well. Stepping to the counter, he made a show of studying his watch as the burly proprietor walked over. "Excuse me," Bolan said. "Do you speak English?"

"Little bit," the man replied.

"I was supposed to meet someone here but I think I'm too late. Maybe you saw him. A tall man, probably wearing a gray suit—"

"*Oui,*" the owner said. "He here. Just leave. But he look for three, how you say, punks. Three men who make much trouble all the time."

"I did miss him, then. Thanks." He nodded and departed. His hunch had been right. Martel hadn't told

Dorsakov about their little run-in, so Bolan didn't have
to worry about Mrs. Delacroix.

The warrior walked south to the corner and turned
onto the street where she lived. Too late he saw the limo
appear down the block. Caught in the glare of its headlights, he had no choice but to stick his hands in his
pockets, bow his head and walk along as if he had no
cares in the world. The limo prowled slowly toward
him. He kept his gaze to the ground as the vehicle drew
even with him so none of the occupants would get a
good look at his face, but at the same time he watched
it out of the corner of one eye in case they were out for
his blood.

The limo braked.

Bolan halted, his right hand creeping toward the Desert Eagle. If they were there to kill him, he would make
a point of nailing the Russian before they took him
down. A man with a deep voice addressed him in accented French. He couldn't just walk on without
arousing suspicion, so he turned but tried to keep his
face in shadow.

The speaker was Mikhail Dorsakov. The rear window was open and his elbow leaned out. He repeated
himself, his brow knitting.

Smiling sheepishly, Bolan went into his tourist act.
"Were you talking to me, mister? I'm afraid my French
isn't what it should be. What do you need?"

The Russian's features were as hard as his soul. There
was no real warmth in them at all, not even when he returned the warrior's smile. His mouth curled briefly,
but the smile didn't reach his cheeks, which resembled
round polished stones, or his eyes, which were like
matched pieces of flint. "You are American, I take it?"
he said in English.

"On vacation," Bolan replied, and thought fast to come up with a cover the KGB alumnus might fall for. "I've climbed just about every other mountain range in Europe and thought it was time I tried the Pyrenees." He paused. "Do you live around here? Do you do any climbing yourself?"

"No on both counts," Dorsakov said suavely, "although I hear that some climbers rate the Pyrenees as first-rate." He raked Bolan from head to toe. "I am sorry to trouble you, but I am looking for three associates of mine, three young men from Paris. Perhaps you have seen them? They drive a yellow sports car."

"I've seen the car a few times," Bolan acknowledged. "It would be hard to miss."

Dorsakov's mouth twitched again. "Very true. Young men often are drawn to flash over substance." He drummed his fingers once on the side of the limo. "May I ask when it was that you saw them last?"

"This morning, before I went off to scout climbing locations," Bolan answered.

The rogue's frown was genuine. "I suppose I should have known better than to hire boys to do a man's job," he said, half to himself. "They probably got themselves lost." His arm withdrew. "Thank you for your time."

Bolan made no move to go on until after the limo vanished around the block. He had no idea whether Dorsakov had believed his lies. The best he could do was keep his fingers crossed.

The Executioner made a circuit of the house before turning in. The lights in the house were out so he let himself in quietly and went straight to bed. Tomorrow promised to be another busy day.

THE FRAGRANT AROMA of perking coffee woke him at sunrise. He shaved, showered and hurried to the Jeep before Mrs. Delacroix could invite him in for a cup.

Even though the hour was early, there were a lot of people abroad. Bolan roamed the streets, seeking a store that sold sporting goods. There was none. He wanted fishing line, but had to settle for two spools of yarn from a small market that carried a few sewing supplies.

The journey to the cutoff was uneventful. When Bolan got there, he drove so he could scan the ridge. No vehicle was parked there. He pulled off the road at the same spot he had the day before. Instead of the camouflage fatigues, the Executioner donned a combat blacksuit. Before setting off he ate a can of beef stew, cold, and a can of peaches. It would be his last meal for a while.

The warrior took his time hiking to the knoll and didn't arrive there until after noon. He broke out the binoculars and settled down to await nightfall. Nothing had changed at the château except that the cars were parked in a different order.

The hours passed slowly. Now and then Bolan saw men moving about indoors. At three in the afternoon a blue van arrived. Dorsakov personally greeted the two occupants, a man and a woman, Mediterraneans by the look of them. The Russian escorted his new guests back through the maze. Bolan tried to keep track of them, but the hedge was too high.

Lights came on both inside and out well before the sun set, the grounds illuminated by the harsh glare of a dozen big spotlights. Then a husky man in a chauffeur's uniform stepped from a side door leading three Dobermans by a single leash. He walked the dogs to the maze entrance, unhooked them and stood back while they trotted in among the thickets.

Bolan's jaw muscles tightened. The warrior had no quarrel with animals performing the tasks they were trained by man to do. Unfortunately he hadn't come prepared to deal with guard dogs. Had he known of their presence, he would have requested a tranquilizer gun to be part of his gear. As it was, if a dog attacked him, he would have to shoot it.

At eight that evening windows on the upper floor lighted up. Through the Starlite scope Bolan saw a spacious chamber in the center of which stood a long table. He had a fleeting glimpse because moments later the chauffeur went from window to window drawing the curtains shut.

The auction would soon be underway.

It was time for the Executioner to ply his trade. He snaked down the knoll and glided through the trees until he was at a point directly across from the outside maze entrance. Up close he could see how badly overgrown the thickets had become, which would only make them harder to negotiate.

On his stomach Bolan wormed his way through a narrow strip of high weeds to the maze. He crouched at the base of the outer thicket, opened his backpack and withdrew one of the balls of yarn. Stalking into the opening, he tied the end of the yarn to a branch tightly enough to insure it wouldn't come loose. Then, the ball in one hand, the M-16 tucked against his side in the other, he advanced stealthily.

Bolan contrived to hold the yarn so that the ball turned with every step, unfurling of its own accord. Now, no matter how deeply into the maze he penetrated, no matter how many blind alleys he found himself in, he would always be able to find his way out again.

At the first corner the warrior stopped and gave the yarn an experimental tug to see if it would hold. It did. He listened for the Dobermans but didn't hear them. It would have made things simple if he could peer over the top of the hedgerow, but the tangled wall of vegetation reared a good eight feet into the air.

The Executioner continued into the maze, pausing often to probe with his senses. Frequently he put an ear to hedges he happened to be passing. Once he heard the heavy panting of one of the Dobermans. It was going in the other direction, obviously didn't scent him and didn't slow down.

The first turn that Bolan took wound up being a dead end. He went back and took another branch. Two turns later he again came up against a solid green wall. So once more he returned to the junction and tried a different avenue.

On and on it went. For every short stretch that took Bolan nearer to the château, he went down five or six dead ends. Several times the yarn snagged on corners and he had to go back and free it.

Bolan was no more than a third of the way into the maze when he heard an ominous growl behind the hedge to his right. He promptly froze, hoping the dog would wander off. Instead, it sniffed loudly and had to have picked up his scent because it growled again, louder this time. He heard it paw at the wall, then pad off.

He knew it was coming for him. And since the dogs were more than likely let loose in the maze every night, it was safe to assume they knew their way around. The one that had smelled him would be on him in no time.

He moved close to the opposite hedge, crouched and drew the Beretta. The Desert Eagle and M-16 both had more stopping power but silence was called for and only the 9 mm pistol had a silencer.

The Doberman wasted no time. In thirty seconds Bolan spied a sleek black shape bounding across the grass toward him. Head low, teeth exposed, the Doberman came on with a low, rumbling snarl, its sleek body a literal blur.

The Executioner fired the Beretta when the dog was ten yards off. He knew he scored a solid hit, yet the Doberman barely broke stride. He fired twice more and the dog buckled and rolled, coming to a stop inches from his leg.

The warrior quickly replaced the spent rounds and holstered the pistol. He resumed his march through the maze, going slower now. There was a good chance the other dogs had heard the commotion and were coming for him.

Ten minutes went by but the Dobermans didn't appear. Bolan found himself at another dead end. He went back to the junction and tried again with the same aggravating result.

The big man stopped and thought out the problem. The walls weren't sturdy enough for him to climb over, or he would. He couldn't smash through them, either, unless he had a chain saw.

He remembered watching the Russian escort the last arrivals inside. The high hedge had hidden them from view, but it seemed to him that they had made the trip in much shorter time than the size of the maze would allow. How could that be when there were so many twists, turns and long passages? he wondered. Was there a secret passage that ran straight through? Or was it just a matter of taking the most direct route? He recalled that the outer entrance to the maze was to the left of the château, and it gave him an idea.

Bolan started winding the yarn. He planned to retrace his steps to the entrance and start over. Moments later he heard a fierce growling that ended as abruptly as it began. The warrior slung the M-16 over his right shoulder and drew the Beretta in case the dog was on his scent. He wound a few more yards of yarn and the line suddenly went slack. Quickening his pace, he kept winding until seconds later, at a junction, he came to the end of the line. The yarn had been cut.

The warrior figured one of the dogs was to blame. He searched the other two branches for the other end of the severed line, but found no trace of it. His ploy had backfired. He was stranded in the middle of the maze.

Bolan was too seasoned a combat vet to let the setback worry him. He would find his way out. None of the branches he had to choose from looked familiar, so he picked one on a whim. It ended at another wall.

The time factor was becoming crucial. Bolan hurried. Turn by turn he made steady headway and seemed to be nearing the outer wall. Then he walked around a bend—and faced one of the Dobermans not five feet away, standing there as if it had been waiting for him. The moment he stepped into sight, it sprang.

So swift was the attack that Bolan was unable to get off a shot before the animal reached him. He did get his left arm up, and the Doberman went for it. Jaws capable of crushing bone crunched down, and had he not deftly twisted and torn the arm loose before the dog's teeth could dig in deep, he would have lost the use of the arm, perhaps for good. As it was, the Doberman ripped the sleeve of the skinsuit and gouged furrows in his flesh.

The dog, though, was not to be denied. It bit again but missed by a hair, its teeth snapping together.

Bolan backed away to keep the Doberman from getting a grip and to give himself room to use the Beretta. The guard dog pressed him, lunging at his left hand. In sheer reflex he let go of the ball of yarn, and as it fell the Doberman snatched it and shook it as if it were Bolan's neck. For a few moments it was distracted, and that was all it took for the warrior to core its brain with a well-placed shot.

The warrior reclaimed the ball, stepped over the twitching animal and hastened on. He soon found the trail of yarn he had left and began winding it around the ball. It brought him to the entrance in no time.

The château lay quiet under the starlight. In the upper chamber the lights were still burning, the auction apparently still in progress. Bolan took a fix on the approximate spot where the inner opening into the maze was located and went back in. This time he turned right at every junction, no matter how many branches there were. His hopes rose as he covered dozens of yards and didn't encounter a single dead end.

Finally Bolan reached the inner opening. He squatted beside it and studied the château. No guards were present, nor was there any movement within. He set down the yarn, then tucked the Starlite scope to his eyes. As before, the perimeter grid was plain to see. A latticework of laser beams crisscrossed the grass strip. Breaking any one of them would set off an alarm.

The Executioner edged into the open, flattened, and made for the nearest door, the M-16 in front of him so he could see through the scope as he worked his way along. He avoided the first beam easily enough, but slowed when confronted by several that shot across the strip at different angles. By contorting himself just right, he slid past them and paused in a narrow space clear of beams.

It was then that Bolan heard two disturbing sounds. The first was the unmistakable noise of a car door closing, which puzzled him. He hadn't heard another vehicle drive up. But before he could give the mystery much thought, he heard another sound that posed a more immediate problem. It was the growl of the third Doberman, and it came from near the maze entrance.

Bolan peered through the scope and crawled quickly, skirting one beam and ducking under another. He was two-thirds of the way across the strip when the growl was repeated, only much louder, much clearer. The warrior looked up and reached for the Beretta.

The last dog stood framed in the gap in the hedgerows. Lip curled up over its wicked fangs, it took a few steps.

The warrior was in a tight spot. If the dog went for him, it would trigger the system and bring every terrorist in the place down on his head. And the alarm might prompt Mikhail Dorsakov to flee with the vials. He had to neutralize the animal quickly. But even as Bolan extended the Beretta, the Doberman stepped farther into the grass. He shifted his eye to the scope and discovered the dog was four or five inches from a beam. As he looked at the animal, it snarled and started toward him.

At the very instant that the Executioner's mission stood
in jeopardy, fate intervened. Bolan heard a muffled
noise from deep within the maze. So did the Doberman. It halted in midstep and tilted its head to hear
better. Then, legs flying, it whirled and dashed back
through the opening.

Bolan had no idea who or what had made the noise
or why the dog had seen fit to run back into the maze
instead of attacking him. But he wasn't about to look a
gift horse in the mouth, as it were. Turning, he wriggled past the last of the laser beams and rose within
several feet of the door.

It wasn't locked. The warrior eased the door inward,
wary the hinges would creak, and found himself in a
wide corridor with plush carpet. At the far end was a
larger door, which was closed. Bolan hurried forward,
heard nothing to indicate anyone was on the other side,
and worked the metal latch.

A stone staircase led upward, and Bolan ascended
them cautiously. He checked with the scope and verified Dorsakov hadn't installed a similar security system in the dank stairwell.

The drone of a man's voice wafted downward. Bolan thought it might be Dorsakov's but couldn't be sure
until he came to the third floor. A dimly lighted hall-

way brought him to a pair of closed polished doors. It had to be the meeting room.

Bolan could hear the Russian clearly. Dorsakov was speaking English, the one language most of the terrorists were bound to have a smattering of. He eavesdropped.

"—that we have all enjoyed our meal and wine, it is time we attend to the matter at hand. You all know why you are here. The bidding will start at one million dollars. American dollars, that is. Who wants to start?"

"One million?" a gruff voice sputtered. "You must be joking. How many of us do you think have access to such a large sum?"

"All of you do, Mr. Basuli," Dorsakov replied. "I have done my research. I only contacted organizations or individuals such as yourself who have the financial resources to meet my minimum bid." The Russian renegade paused. "I trust we will not bandy words in this regard. All of you must have known that the bidding would start high. This is a once-in-a-lifetime opportunity. Whoever buys the Novichok-5 will possess the deadliest biochemical weapon ever conceived. Think of it. Think of the havoc you could wreak. No one would dare stand up to you for fear of having the weapon used against them. You would have power such as few have ever had since the dawn of time."

Bolan heard murmuring. Someone else spoke up.

"You were in the wrong line of work with the KGB, Mikhail. You should have moved to a capitalist country and made your living as a salesman of real estate or expensive cars. You would have made your million long ago."

A few people laughed lightly.

"So which one of you will start the bidding?" Dorsakov prompted. "I need not remind you that the sooner we get this over with, the better for all of us. I am a wanted man. There is no telling how long we have before my hiding place is discovered."

"Not so fast," someone said. "I think you try to rush us. I, for one, want proof we do not waste our money. I would like to see the Novichok-5."

"Only the high bidder gets to see the vials, Anastasius," Dorsakov said. "That was made clear to you when I first contacted your group."

"Is the Novichok-5 here?" Anastasius asked.

"Surely you don't expect me to answer such a question?" the Russian replied. "Where it is or isn't is none of your concern. Now let's get down to business. I have already discussed the bidding with our Japanese friends and they are—"

Bolan didn't stay to hear any more. He had to find the vials, and to that end he hurried to the stairs and down to the second floor. Finding the vials would be like looking for a needle in a haystack, he knew, only worse. They could be almost anywhere.

Bolan had one helpful clue. According to Intel acquired by Brognola, at the time of its theft the Novichok-5 was contained in a special shatterproof case. The big Fed hadn't been able to learn its size, its shape, or anything else other than the case was metal. The warrior doubted that Dorsakov had removed the vials. Tampering with Novichok-5 was like playing Russian roulette with a revolver that had bullets in all six chambers. Odds were that the case was at the château, somewhere. His best bet, he felt, was to locate Dorsakov's bedroom.

It proved to be easier planned than done. The château was huge, boasting forty-one rooms. He'd located the bedchambers and ran from one to the other, rummaging through drawers and looking in closets. The first five he entered were unlocked. The sixth, though, was locked, which gave him hope that it might be the right one.

All of the château's doors had latches, not knobs. Although Bolan strained against the latch and put his shoulder to the locked door, it wouldn't budge. He could kick it in, but the noise was bound to bring Dorsakov and the terrorists. Then he remembered the key he had taken from Jules Martel.

It took only a few moments to remove the key from the backpack and insert it in the lock. Bolan twisted and heard the rasp of tumblers. The heavy door swung inward at his push. He immediately saw that the room didn't belong to Mikhail Dorsakov. On the bed lay a pair of leather pants that matched the jacket Martel had worn. The room had belonged to the Parisians.

Bolan started to back out. He thought it best to leave the door as he had found it, so he reached for the latch. Doing so saved his life. From down the corridor came the chug of a silencer and a slug thudded into the panel above his head. He threw himself into the room, spun and pressed against the jamb.

The husky chauffeur was partially concealed by the stairs, where the wall ended. He held a pistol in both hands, and when Bolan chanced a look out, the driver snapped off a shot that showed he was a competent marksman. The bullet tore into the wood within a finger's width of the Executioner's face.

Bolan drew the Beretta and fired twice, driving the man from sight. He expected the chauffeur would give a yell at any second to bring the men upstairs on the run. Since he had been discovered, there was no longer any need to rely on stealth. He could confront the terrorists head-on and do what he did best. The vials would just have to wait.

Suddenly the château was rocked by a tremendous explosion below. The blast was so strong that the floor under Bolan's feet quivered. Billowing clouds of dust and debris gusted up the stairs, enveloping the chauffeur.

Bolan didn't know what to make of it. He speculated the French authorities had learned Dorsakov was at the château and launched an assault, but it seemed strange they would do so in such a reckless manner. Then he heard yells and the rapid-fire chatter of submachine guns. Above and below him a great commotion broke out. A battle royal was being waged, and he was stuck in the middle.

He dashed across the corridor into another bedroom, and over to a window that afforded a view of the driveway and the front of the château. There were no military or police vehicles, no helicopters, no soldiers or police. The driveway was as he had last seen it, except that the side door on the van was open. He turned to go, then spotted someone moving along the inner wall of the hedge. It was a man in a black ski mask, dressed in a black shirt and pants and carrying a carbine of some sort.

Bolan ran to the hall. Dust still swirled at the far end. On the third floor the automatic fire had reached a crescendo. Men were shouting, screaming and cursing. Since the only way out was by the stairs, the warrior headed for them, keeping close to the wall. He held the

M-16 in both hands and had the selector lever on full-auto.

The chauffeur was gone. Bolan had a choice to make. Should he go up, after Dorsakov, or go down and lie low until the battle was over and he could sort out the players?

Unexpectedly another man in a ski mask loomed out of the gloom. He was armed with a Valmet military rifle, its folding stock tucked to his right shoulder. The moment he set eyes on the warrior, he spun to fire.

Bolan was quicker. He stroked the trigger, and the M-16 unleashed its metallic litany of death, pockmarking the gunner's face and chest with bright red splotches. The man tumbled down the stairs without uttering a word, followed by Bolan. The bottom part of the staircase was a shattered wreck, and he had to pick his way over the jumbled debris to reach the buckled corridor. He guessed that whoever set off the blast had intended to trap Dorsakov and the terrorists on the upper floors. A few more pounds of explosive and they would have succeeded. The stairs would have been completely demolished.

The warrior sprinted for the exit. He passed a room with the door wide open and spotted another armed ski-masked hardman bent over a computer console. Reversing direction, he aimed at the gunner as the man turned toward him. A light squeeze of the trigger was all it took to stitch the man from crotch to chin.

The display on the computer monitor was in Russian. Bolan had learned enough of the Cyrillic alphabet over the years to make an educated guess that before him was part of a file on a terrorist organization. He popped out a floppy disk and stuck it in a pocket. On a table beside the computer sat a disk storage box that was filled with disks. He quickly crammed them into his backpack and was zipping it when footsteps pounded up the stairs.

Bolan sped to the door and put his back to the wall. A pair of men in ski masks raced past on their way to the outer door. He stepped out and said "Hey!" As they began to turn, he cut them down. Then he raced for the outer door.

Another gigantic blast shook the château as the big man broke into the clear. He crossed the grass to the maze and stopped just inside it to look back.

Smoke poured from a dozen windows, and flames were visible in a dozen more. The sound of gunfire had tapered but not yet died out.

The warrior jogged to the outer opening and headed for the knoll. He had passed the last hedge when an engine coughed to life down by the river. Changing course, he ran the length of the maze and saw a small dock. Next to it was a trim speedboat. At the controls was Mikhail Dorsakov. Bolan raised the M-16 and started forward, but as he went past the corner a dark shape leapt out at him. The warrior tried to turn. He caught a glimpse of the husky chauffeur and of a gun barrel streaking at his skull.

Then the world went black.

SCORES OF MILES AWAY, at the nearest airstrip to the château, Hal Brognola paced in front of a portable radio console, an unlit cigar wedged in the corner of his mouth. "Anything yet?" he asked the operator.

"No, sir," the man responded.

Brognola stepped outside into the cool night and tried to tell himself that he shouldn't be worried. Bolan had undertaken too many hazardous missions to count, and always survived. His friend had an uncanny knack in that regard. But Brognola couldn't stop himself from fretting. This time was different. This time they were dealing with a biochemical agent so toxic that a single drop unleashed into the air was capable of killing countless people over a wide area, including Bolan.

That was only part of the reason Brognola worried. The other part had to do with being forced to send Bolan into a hostile situation with his hands tied, so to speak. Earlier, against October Dawn, he had insisted the warrior take one or two of them alive, knowing that doing so put the Executioner at a grave disadvantage. Now he had hamstrung his friend again by asking him to hold back until the Novichok-5 was secured.

The big Fed paced again. It annoyed him a bit that he was so upset. He would have thought that after so many years of overseeing sensitive operations, he would have a tighter rein on his emotions. His stomach was twisted into a knot.

Minutes later the radio operator shouted, "Sir! Message for you!"

Brognola hurried into the hangar. It was an intelligence report from the man he had left in charge in Marseilles. Several members of a terrorist group known as the Silver Crescent, which had strong ties to Libya, had been seen getting off a jet at the Marseilles airport. They had been shadowed to a downtown hotel where they were joined by seven others. All of them had then piled into a brown van. Not long after they had shaken their tail.

The Justice man was perplexed by the news. So far as he knew, the Silver Crescent hadn't been one of the organizations Dorsakov had invited to the auction. They were hotheads who killed for the thrill of it, the very worst of the worst. What were they doing in France, now, of all times? It couldn't be coincidence. Brognola looked at the message again. The van had eluded the two agents shortly before noon. That meant it could have reached the château hours ago.

Maybe the Russian had invited them after all, Brognola mused, last-minute replacements for October Dawn. The capture of Berta Stein had been a top news story and made all the papers. Dorsakov was bound to have heard.

There were too many unknown factors to suit Brognola. He wished Bolan would radio in to report everything had gone according to plan and the Novichok-5 had been recovered.

Moving to the doorway, he gazed at the two helicopters waiting for the word to lift off. Cooling their heels inside the choppers were two dozen agents armed to the teeth. All he needed to get them rolling was word from Striker.

"Mack," the big Fed said softly to himself, "wherever the hell you are, I hope you're all right."

As BOLAN FELT HIMSELF regaining consciousness, he didn't reveal the fact by opening his eyes or moving a muscle. He lay still and listened. The throaty growl of the speedboat engine told him where he was. He could feel the rolling motion of the craft as it sped down the river. Light spray spattered his face every so often.

The warrior cracked his eyelids. Sitting at the wheel, with his back to him, was Dorsakov. Bolan lay on the floor between seats. Without having to feel for them, he knew the Beretta and the Desert Eagle were gone. But not the backpack. Glancing to his left, he saw the chauffeur seated quietly on the other seat, smirking at him, holding a Walther P-5 pointed at his head. The chauffeur addressed Dorsakov in Russian without looking up.

"He is awake, Mikhail, but pretending not to be."

The motor slowed from a whine to a rumble. The former KGB agent swiveled and regarded the warrior critically. "You can open your eyes, American. Roskov is never wrong about such things."

Bolan did as he was told. "Can I sit up?" It was cramped between the seats, and he wanted room to maneuver.

"Be my guest," Dorsakov said suavely. "But move quite slowly or Roskov will shoot you in the eye before you can blink. He is quite protective of me."

"Your personal pit bull," Bolan said while easing upward. He braced his shoulders against the side of the boat and tucked his legs to his chest.

"Pit bull?" Dorsakov said. "Oh. I see. An attempt at humor." He draped an arm on the back of his seat. "Why is it that you Americans feel compelled to make a joke about everything? I was in your country a few times and saw some of your television. Nearly every show was the same. People making jokes at the expense of other people. It was cruel, not funny. Yet the audiences laughed and laughed."

Bolan could think of nothing more ridiculous than getting into a conversation about the merits of sitcoms with a renegade Russian in the middle of a remote river in France, so he said nothing.

"I am not surprised to see you again," Dorsakov went on. "I knew you were not a mountain climber."

"What gave me away?" Bolan asked. He didn't understand why the Russians had spared him but imagined he would soon find out.

"Oh, you played the part of a typical American oaf quite nicely," Dorsakov said. "But I have been in the business too long not to know a competitor when I see one. I suppose I should have had you killed, but I knew if I did, your government would know that I knew I was being watched. As well, it was too late to cancel my auction with most of those I had invited already here."

Bolan glanced at the man in the chauffeur's uniform, hoping he would lower his guard, but the arms that held the Walther were rock steady.

"Above all else I did not want my auction interrupted," Dorsakov said, then sighed. "As it turned out, my concern was misplaced. I never should have trusted them."

"Who?" Bolan asked. He noticed there were no lights along either bank of the river. The two Russians could kill him, hide his body on shore or sink it to the bottom, and no one would ever learn his fate.

Dorsakov ignored the question. "Roskov could easily have shot you back at the château. You must be wondering why I have spared your life."

"It did cross my mind."

"Because I want you to deliver a message to your superiors. Advise them to pass on the same message to the other governments whose hounds are nipping at my heels."

"What sort of message?"

The renegade leaned toward the console, and his arm dipped. When he raised it again, he was holding what appeared to be a metal attaché case. "Do you know what this is?"

Bolan had known the instant he set eyes on it. "The Novichok-5."

"You have done your homework," Dorsakov said. He cradled the case in one arm and stroked it with his other hand, as he might caress a lover. "Do you know what this means to me?"

"A million dollars."

"I'm sure I will receive more than that," Dorsakov said brusquely. "But I was not referring to the money." He reverently set the case down. "Novichok-5 will give me the means to live the rest of my days in luxury. The best food, the prettiest women, a fine estate, I will have it all."

Bolan couldn't help but think of Joseph, the turncoat German agent. Greed was one of the oldest of mankind's vices, but it never failed to find new converts. "You can enjoy all that if you can find someplace on earth where you'll be safe," he commented. "Half the police agencies in the world want your head, and they're not about to stop looking even if you sell the Novichok-5."

"True enough," Dorsakov said. "Happily I have that problem all worked out. For a hefty sum I will be granted asylum in a country where no other government can touch me."

Bolan looked at him. "You're smart enough to know they'll get you sooner or later. Your own people will hunt you down in time, if no one else does."

The Russian nodded sadly. "They will. But it doesn't matter. I will have beaten the system at its own game. I will have shown them that putting me out in the cold was the wrong thing for them to do."

"You were no longer with Russian Intelligence when you stole the vials?" Bolan asked. "Your people told ours—"

"Since when has my government ever told the truth about anything?" Dorsakov cut him off. "You have no doubt learned that I worked for the KGB. But did you know I was cut loose when the KGB was restructured? I was supposedly too hard-line for those who took over." Dorsakov paused, his face reddening. "Me!" he cried, thumping his chest. "Who gave his life to the KGB! Who shunned family and friends for the greater glory of my country! And look at how I was treated."

The revelation surprised the warrior. It put Dorsakov's actions in a whole new light. Greed didn't enter into the picture. Dorsakov's true motive was revenge. "You're right," he said. "We weren't told."

"Nor would my government admit it if you presented them with the facts. But enough about me. I want you to carry a message, and it is this." He leaned over the seat so his face was close to Bolan's. "Tell them, American, that I am weary of being hounded. Tell them that I have changed my plans. I still intend to sell the Novichok-5 to the highest bidder. But there are four vials in the case. I can easily sell three and still make a fortune."

Bolan saw where the statements were leading and felt the vague chill again.

"Warn them, American, that if I am hounded just one more time, I will unleash one of the vials in a major city. Make sure they appreciate the consequences."

"They will."

The Russian straightened. "I hope so, for their sakes and for the sake of all those who will die if they try anything." His voice softened. "I do not want to kill innocents, but if left no choice, I will. No doubt my government made me out to be a cold-blooded madman, yet nothing could be further from the truth. Yes,

I've killed before, but always in the line of duty. Yes, I've done other terrible things, but again, always in the line of duty. Just as you have, I would imagine. Does that make me more evil than you?''

Bolan had no answer. Dorsakov was more complex than he had been led to believe, but that didn't make him any less dangerous. He looked down at his feet, debating what to say, and suddenly was seized by the left arm and propelled over the side. He twisted as he fell, dived cleanly and went under. The cold water brought a chill of its own. Kicking hard, he surfaced and saw the speedboat racing into the gloom. Roskov stood and watched him, the pistol leveled.

The darkness had almost swallowed the craft when a shout from Mikhail Dorsakov wafted on the wind. "Remember, American! Warn them! Make them believe you, or many thousands will die!"

The big man trod water as the sound of the engine dwindled in the night.

8

As soon as the sun rose, Mack Bolan and Hal Brognola made an inspection of the heavily damaged château. In addition to two large holes blown in the outer walls, the fire and gunfire had taken a heavy toll. Most walls were dotted with bullet holes, and half the windows had been shot out. Furniture lay in shattered pieces. Paintings had been reduced to scrap.

"It's a pity," Brognola said as they walked along the third-floor hall. "There aren't many old châteaus like this one left. The French will complain we bungled the job."

Bolan had more important matters on his mind than a local landmark. "What's the latest on our friend?"

"There's been no word. He slipped through the net we set up and is long gone by now." Brognola stopped to watch his men attend to several bodies. "He's clever like a fox, this one."

"We have no idea at all where he went?"

"I might," Brognola said. "I'm expecting a report within the hour, and I'll fill you in once I receive it."

"What about the disks I recovered?" Bolan asked.

"Your guess was on the money. They're his files on various terrorist groups, but they tell us little new information and give no clues at all to his current whereabouts."

Bolan was disappointed. Since contacting the big Fed in the wee hours of the morning he had been hoping for a break that would lead them to Dorsakov quickly. "What about those guys in the black ski masks?"

"Guys and women," Brognola corrected him. "We found a dead female in the same outfit." He pulled a sheet of paper from an inner pocket and unfolded it. "From the positive identification made on two of them, we believe they were all members of the Silver Crescent."

"Isn't that one of the Libyan front groups?"

"It is. The way I read it is this." Brognola stopped beside the corpse of a black-haired man being tucked into a body bag. "Dorsakov invited the Silver Crescent to sit in on his auction, but they decided they could have their cake and eat it, too."

"They tried to snatch the vials rather than pay for them," Bolan guessed.

"Precisely. Only our fox of a friend was too smart for them. He took a secret passage out the back and got away while the Silver Crescent was busy fighting the other terrorists." Brognola moved aside as the body bag was carted off. "I can't think of anything more fitting than having terrorists kill other terrorists. Too bad we can't toss all of them into a big arena and let them finish each other off."

"What's the final tally?"

Brognola checked his sheet. "Six members of the Silver Crescent were killed, which leaves four on the loose somewhere. The Red Dragons delegates won't be returning to Japan. One of the Popular Liberation Front members was killed, one from the Burning Light and five others we have yet to identify."

"And Roskov?"

"Was only posing as a chauffeur. His full name is Sergei Bilibin Roskovich. He's another KGB alumnus. Evidently he worked for years under Dorsakov and resigned about the time Dorsakov claims he was forced to step down."

They walked into the meeting room, which was in a shambles. Dry blood dotted the floor, red splotches marked the walls and ceiling. Brognola looked around in disgust. "The Silver Crescent pinned most of the others down in here. It must have been a bloodbath."

Bolan stepped to a shattered window and stared out at the Pyrenees. A few of the peaks were crowned with snow which gleamed like gemstones in the bright morning sunlight. He looked lower, at the maze, and thought of the third Doberman, found with six bullet holes in its head. Apparently it had tried to stop the Silver Crescent hit squad from reaching the château. "What now, Hal?"

"Well, there is one item I haven't mentioned yet," Brognola said.

The warrior cocked an inquiring brow.

"Another helicopter is due in any minute. On it will be your temporary partner."

"My what?"

"Hear me out," Brognola said. "The President has relayed a request from the Russians. They want one of their own people in on the hunt from here on out."

"No," Bolan said. After everything Dorsakov had told him, he was unwilling to trust the Russians.

"The President would be grateful if you went along on this one. The Russian president made the request personally. They're sending one of their top operatives, someone who has worked with Dorsakov before and knows his habits. Someone who can pick him out of a crowd, if need be."

"I can do that now that I've seen him," Bolan said.

"It's up to you," Brognola said. "I won't push. But it might be in our best interest to accept. Maybe this agent of theirs can help us nab Dorsakov that much sooner."

"Is he Russian Intelligence?"

"They wouldn't say. Only that it's one of their best."

Bolan would have liked some time to weigh the pros and cons, but at that moment the sound of an approaching chopper lifted his eyes to the eastern sky where a Mil Mi-17, a top-of-the-line Russian helicopter, was arcing in out of the sun to set down next to the helicopters Brognola and his men had arrived in. There was another chopper there, too, a sleek French Gazelle that had brought in the French government's liaison, a bantam rooster named Bouvier.

"It wouldn't hurt to meet the man," Brognola suggested, motioning the Executioner to join him.

Bolan fell into step beside the big Fed, and they descended to ground level. As they turned the corner into the hall leading to the main entrance, one of Brognola's men briskly opened the door and stepped back as if to admit royalty. When the warrior saw why, he stopped in his tracks and was aware his companion had done the same.

Into the château strolled an Amazon of a woman in an expensive suit. She had a mane of rich brown hair that fell well past her shoulders. Her face was as smooth as glass, her eyes the color of the sea. Shoulders back, hands stiff at her sides as if she were marching on parade, she walked right up to them. "Mr. Brognola, I believe," she said in clipped English. "I recognize you from the photo I was shown. I am Marya Kuragin. I believe you are expecting me.''

Rarely had Bolan seen Brognola speechless, but the big Fed appeared to be at a complete loss for words. Apparently the higher-ups had sprung a surprise on him, as well. Bolan offered his hand. "I'm Mike Belasko. I believe you're expecting to work with me.''

"I am looking forward to it," Kuragin said, giving him a firm handshake. "For the sake of both our countries, I want to see this cold-blooded madman caught."

Bolan kept his face impassive. Those had been the exact words Dorsakov had used. He wondered if the woman really knew him, or whether she was nothing more than a political assassin sent to stamp out a source of embarrassment to her government.

"This is for you," the woman said, handing a file to Brognola. "My credentials are all in order."

"I would imagine they are," the Justice man replied. He extended his own hand and was impressed by her strength. Under that suit were muscles of steel.

"Have you located the traitor yet?" Kuragin asked.

"Not yet, but we're working on it," Brognola said. "In fact, I need to check if any messages have come in. If you'll excuse me, I'll leave you in Mr. Belasko's capable hands."

Marya Kuragin studied the warrior as if he were a fashion model on display. "Why are there mud stains on your clothes, Mr. Belasko?"

"It's a long story. And call me Mike. Care to stretch your legs after your long flight?"

"I would be grateful for the exercise."

There were agents loading bodies into ambulances, agents cleaning up the lawn, agents guarding the choppers, and every last one of them stared when the Russian operative emerged. Bolan couldn't blame them. He had met some real beauties in his time, but none as stunning as the woman at his side. "What are your orders?" he asked bluntly.

"To assist you in every way possible. I am at Mr. Brognola's disposal."

So far, so good, Bolan reflected, but was she sincere or parroting words provided by her superiors? "I'll be honest with you. I prefer to work alone."

"As do I. But for the good of both our countries and all those who will suffer if the Novichok-5 is ever used, I think we must each sacrifice our personal desires."

"You don't mind working with me?"

The woman halted. "Since you have been honest with me, I will be honest with you. Yes, I resent being ordered to take orders from Americans. But I am a patriot. What my country asks of me, I will do. I think you would do no less."

Her words were said with passion, but Bolan noted that the passion didn't light up her eyes. Either she *was* being a parrot, or she had her emotions under perfect control. "If we were to corner Dorsakov, and I was to tell you that I wanted him alive, what would you do?"

"Alive?" A chink appeared in her robot exterior, and she showed genuine surprise. "Why would you want to take a lunatic like him alive?"

Just then the front door to the château burst outward, and Hal Brognola hurried toward them, waving a message in the air. "Pack your bags, kids. I think I know where we can find the Novichok-5."

PARIS, FRANCE. The City of Light. One of the major cities of the world. Home to the Eiffel Tower, the Arc de Triomphe, the Louvre.

Mack Bolan had passed through Paris many times. He knew the city better than he knew most big cities, and he didn't find it at all surprising that Brognola believed Mikhail Dorsakov had gone to ground there.

The big Fed's reasoning was solid, in Bolan's view.

For one thing, it was unlikely Dorsakov would try to flee the country anytime soon. The French government had, in effect, thrown a cordon around France. All flights out were being closely but discreetly monitored, as were ships and trains. Every policeman in France was on the lookout for the rogue, and special agents had been assigned to all highway checkpoints.

Since Dorsakov had used an old KGB safehouse, the château, for his big meet, Brognola felt it likely that the Russian had taken refuge in another. And there were known to be several in Paris.

The third factor was Dorsakov's threat. He had warned that he would use one of the vials in a major city, and in France, Paris was *the* city. Many tens of thousands would die if Dorsakov carried out his pledge. He undoubtedly counted on that knowledge to keep those after him at bay.

Finally there was the matter of the three street toughs hired by the Russian to keep unwanted visitors from the château. Brognola had confirmed they hailed from the City of Light and learned that all three had criminal records. It proved that Dorsakov had been to Paris at least once in recent weeks and might well flee to a sanctuary there if pressed.

Bolan reviewed all this in his head as he drove the sedan Brognola had provided from Orly Airport into the metropolis. He had the feeling eyes were on him and glanced at his new "partner," who was studying him intently. "Yes?"

"I was wondering," Kuragin said.

"About what?" The woman had been quiet on the flight from Marseilles, speaking only when spoken to. Brognola had brought her up to speed on the latest developments, and she hadn't asked a single question, which had struck Bolan as strange. It was as if she already knew all that had gone down, or she simply didn't care.

"You. What sort of man you are."

Bolan had to swerve to avoid a compact car that zipped in front of him. It reminded him that Parisian drivers and New York drivers had a lot in common. Driving in either city was a lot like taking part in a demolition derby.

"What I mean," Kuragin elaborated, "is that you were warned by the traitor what would happen if anyone came after him. Yet here you are. Does it not bother you just a little knowing that if Dorsakov finds you are after him, many lives will be lost?"

"Lives will be lost no matter what I do," Bolan said. "If a terrorist group gets its hands on the Novichok-5, they'll use all the vials and the death toll will be a lot higher than if Dorsakov uses only one." A taxi tried to cut him off but he sped past it, causing the driver to veer off or be hit. The taxi driver railed at him and made an obscene gesture.

"So you see yourself as picking the course that is the lesser of two evils?" the woman asked.

"Something like that. Besides, I've seen him, talked to him. Like you, I have a better chance of spotting him than the average *gendarme*."

"How noble of you to risk your life so that many will live."

Bolan couldn't tell if she was being serious or sarcastic. The matter became moot when he glanced in the rearview mirror for the tenth time since leaving Orly and spotted a green four-door that had been behind them the whole way. "We have company," he announced, and was pleased when she didn't jerk around to look as an amateur would have done.

"Who could it be? No one but our own people and the French know we are here."

"I have no idea," Bolan replied, turning right. "But we're not the only players involved. The Silver Crescent wants to get its hands on the Novichok-5. And there are probably others we don't know about."

"Do we lose them?"

"We do." The other car was several blocks back. He came to a side street and abruptly turned into it, his tires screeching. Halfway down the block was an alley, which he entered. He went ten yards, braked and twisted to look out the back.

Ten seconds later the green car flashed past. Four men were inside, and none glanced into the alley.

"Neatly done," Kuragin complimented him as he drove to the end of the alley and took a left to bring them back to the main avenue.

"Lots of practice," Bolan said. He took a sheet of paper from his shirt pocket and showed it to her. "The three addresses listed are all former KGB safehouses. Hal thinks Dorsakov might be holed up in one of them." He looked at her. "Do you know of any others?"

Kuragin read the list aloud, then shook her head and gave the paper back. "No."

"Maybe you should contact your government," Bolan suggested. "Have them get in touch with the intelligence agency."

"There is no need," the woman assured him.

"Why is that?"

"Because I *am* an agent of Russian Intelligence."

"That wasn't in your file."

"Why should it have been?" the woman asked. "The file we were given on you did not mention any agency affiliation. You are not with the CIA, the NSA, the OSI or even with Delta Force. If I am to believe what your government told us, you are a lone wolf they pulled out of thin air, like a rabbit out of a hat. I am not so gullible."

Neither of them said another word until Bolan reached the first KGB haven, a three-story house in the Montmartre section of the city. The warrior cruised past it slowly. The shades had all been drawn, and the house gave every appearance of being abandoned. He pulled to the curb.

"We go in?"

"Yes," Bolan said, taking out the Beretta to check the clip. He saw her reach under her jacket to pull out her own weapon. He thought it would be a small 9 mm or .380 of Russian make. Instead, she pulled out a Grizzly AutoMag, popped out the magazine, inspected it and popped it back in with no wasted motion. She caught him looking at her, and grinned.

"I like stopping power."

"So I see."

Kuragin slid the cannon into its shoulder rig. "I dated a CIA operative once who liked to carry one. It was love at first sight."

"With the guy or the gun?" Bolan asked. Her response was a tight smile.

"The ammo is quite expensive, and all my coats and jackets must be padded to hide the holster, but I never, as those commercials say, leave home without it."

Bolan climbed out and walked to the sidewalk. There were few pedestrians. It was a quiet residential neighborhood flanking the Montmartre cemetery. He went up the steps and stood by the door. Kuragin produced a key, opened the door and boldly entered, her hand under her jacket.

The warrior followed her. He motioned for her to take the downstairs while he took the upstairs. Moving silently to the next floor, he searched from room to room. It was obvious from the dust and dirty windows that no one had stayed there for quite some time.

Bolan went back down. There was no sign of Kuragin, so he moved along the carpeted hall. Halfway to the rear he heard her talking in a low voice. He slowed so she wouldn't hear him and edged toward an open door. Just when her words were distinct enough for him to make them out, a floorboard creaked under his right foot. She promptly stopped talking.

Kuragin was seated at a desk, going through the drawers. She smiled at him as he entered. "I have nothing to indicate the traitor was here. How about you?"

"Zilch." Bolan paused. "I thought I heard you talking to someone."

The woman smiled. "I mumble to myself sometimes. It is a bad habit, I know, but one I have not yet been able to break."

Bolan didn't believe her for a second, but he had no clue as to what she had been up to. "Did you look out back?"

"No. I did not think there was a need."

"You never know," the warrior said. The back door opened onto a short lawn bordered by a wrought-iron fence. Beyond lay the cemetery where row after row of headstones lined the side of a low hill. The lawn was overgrown with grass and weeds, added proof the safehouse hadn't been used in ages.

"Anything?" Kuragin asked when he returned. She was peering behind a wall fixture.

"We're wasting our time. We might as well check out the other two addresses."

"If you say so, but I honestly cannot see the traitor being stupid enough to make the same mistake twice. He is sly, that one. He knows that we will check all the old safehouses, and he will stay away from them."

"Maybe. But it's the only lead we have so let's go." Bolan started to turn.

"Mr. Belasko, wait," Kuragin said. "Before we leave, I would like an answer to the question I asked you back at the château. Why would you even want to take this madman alive?"

"I've got a question of my own," Bolan countered. "Why do you always refer to him as a madman or a traitor? Why don't you ever mention him by name?"

"What difference does it make? He is beneath contempt no matter what I call him. This lunatic holds the city of Paris in the palm of his hand, yet you want to take him alive. It makes no sense, Mr. Belasko."

"Do you know why he stole the Novichok-5?"

"He is insane. It is that simple."

"Did your superiors tell you that they put Dorsakov out to pasture awhile ago?"

"No. Again, what difference does it make? He is deranged, a mass murderer in the making. He must be eliminated before it is too late. Nothing else matters."

Bolan headed for the front door. Twice now he had seen raw hatred in her lovely eyes when the subject of Dorsakov came up. There was more to it than the threat Dorsakov posed, he was certain. And he would find out what.

The warrior opened the front door and stopped. The green four-door had pulled up in front of the house. The doors were thrown open, and four hardmen rushed toward the steps.

9

In the daily life-or-death situations in which the Executioner found himself, reflexes were the name of the game. Those who had the sharpest, lived; those who didn't, died. And the Executioner's were as finely honed as a straight razor.

The two men nearest the house swept hands under their jackets. The warrior didn't wait to see what they pulled out. He slammed the door, threw the bolt and whirled, giving Mayra Kuragin a hard shove. "Out the back way," he said. "Quick."

To her credit the Russian agent didn't argue or ask needless questions. She turned and ran.

Bolan cleared the 93-R from its rig as a heavy blow struck the door. He aimed at the center, figuring they would kick it in. Another resounding blow echoed in the narrow hall as he reached the rear door, which Kuragin held open.

Pointing at the wrought-iron fence, Bolan sprinted across the yard and tried the small gate. It was locked. "Up and over," he directed. Suiting action to words, he replaced the Beretta and climbed. He avoided the spikes at the top and dropped into the cemetery. A thud told him the Russian was at his side.

Rising, Bolan ran to the left. He intended to scale the fence farther down and return unseen to their car, but two of the gunners rushed around the front corner of the house, spied him and Marya, and let out yells to bring the others.

The warrior veered into the virtually empty cemetery and sped toward the top of the hill, intending to carry the fight somewhere innocent bystanders wouldn't be hurt. As he sprinted past a headstone, a slug struck the upper edge and sent slivers flying. Several stung the back of his hand. He looked back and saw three of the gunners scaling the fence. The fourth had a silenced pistol out and was trying to get a bead.

"Why do we not stand and fight?" Kuragin asked, hardly breathing hard from her exertion.

"We will," Bolan promised on the fly. Lining the crown of the hill were dozens of elaborate mausoleums among which they could lose themselves. They were almost there when he glanced around again and saw all four hardmen in pursuit.

Bolan dashed in among the tombs and cut to the right. Kuragin cut to the left but halted on realizing her mistake. Without thinking, the warrior grabbed her hand and pulled her after him, deeper into the crypts. When he judged they had gone far enough, he whipped behind a marble wall topped by stone gargoyles and drew the Beretta.

"At last," the Russian said, doing the same with her Grizzly.

"I'd rather you didn't use that if you can avoid it," Bolan said. "One shot will bring every cop within ten city blocks."

"But it is the only gun I have. How am I supposed to protect myself if I do not use it?"

"I'll handle this. You stay put," the warrior instructed, and could tell she was upset. "If any of them get past me, use your howitzer if you want. But don't blame me if the Paris police haul you in for questioning.'' He headed out before she could protest, running to a particular tomb with carved figures lining all four walls. The figures were easy to climb. Once on the flat roof he moved to the front and crouched.

The quartet of killers weren't long in showing themselves. They were like four peas in a pod; all were stocky, had their hair clipped short and wore ill-fitting suits.

Bolan saw one man motion at the other three and they fanned out. Sighting on the leader, he bided his time until they were in killing range, then caressed the trigger twice. The leader did a pirouette to the ground. One of the others noticed him fall and uttered a shout that sent all three scurrying for cover. The Executioner snapped off a round at the hardman who'd warned his companions, but the guy gained the sanctuary of a large mausoleum.

The warrior waited for one of the gunners to show himself, but they were pros. None did, until a minute later when one materialized under the overhang of a tomb off to the left and pumped several shots in the warrior's direction.

Bolan crawled to the rear wall. Rather than climb and expose himself, he vaulted over the edge and dropped the fifteen feet to the grass. From there he ducked behind another crypt.

The Executioner focused on where he expected one of the trio would appear. Moments passed and one did, bent at the knees as he sidled along a tomb next to the one from which Bolan had opened fired on them. The gunner had eyes only for the mausoleum with all the carved figures. It was a fatal mistake.

Whirling, Bolan headed to the left. If he could get around behind the remaining pair, it would all be over. He hadn't gone far when he saw someone crossing the slope below. He elevated the Beretta but held his fire. It was Marya Kuragin.

The woman saw him, squatted at the base of a tomb and beckoned.

Irritated that she hadn't listened to him, Bolan dashed to her side. He held his tongue for the time being and took the lead, working down to the bottom of the hill and then dashing across the cemetery toward the wrought-iron fence. No angry shouts attended them; no hardmen appeared.

Bolan was first in the car. He gunned the engine as he climbed in and squealed out into the street before she had her door closed. "I don't think much of what you did back there," he said.

"What? You are mad because I did not like being a sitting duck?" Kuragin gave an unladylike snort. "Since you did not want me to defend myself, I decided I would be safer in the car."

"Is that it? Or were you trying to run off and leave me?"

"Why would I do such a thing?"

"I don't know," Bolan replied. "You tell me." He took a turn and accelerated toward a busier thoroughfare. The rearview mirror, so far, was empty.

"If you ask me, Mr. Belasko," Kuragin said coldly, "I would say you have a suspicious nature, too damned suspicious for your own good."

"It's kept me alive this long." He turned onto Rue Caulaincourt and drove toward the center of Paris.

"Where are you going?" the Russian agent asked. "The second safehouse is in west Paris. You are heading north."

"I want to make sure we lost our tail before we visit the next one. And I don't know about you, but I'm hungry. We'll stop at a café for a bite to eat."

"How can you think of food at such a time? A maniac has the means to destroy all life in this city, and all you can think of is your stomach?"

"Afraid so." Bolan had an ulterior motive but he wasn't about to tell her. At the first café they came to, he parked and picked an outdoor table, then excused himself. Going indoors, he made sure she was staying put and went to the phone. In no time he had tapped in the special number and was routed to Brognola.

"How goes it, Striker?" the big Fed asked.

"We hardly got to first base and the opposition showed," Bolan reported.

"Whose team were they on?"

"They weren't wearing uniforms." Bolan glanced at the door, but there was no sign of Kuragin. "That's not why I called. Have you heard anything from your people in Moscow yet?"

"Sorry. No. Give them a few more hours, and we'll know her life history from the day she was born until the minute she arrived in that chopper."

"I'll call you in four," Bolan said, and hung up. He turned, and there she was, coming toward him.

"May I use that now? My superiors have a few contacts in Paris who might know if Dorsakov has shown up."

"Be my guest." The warrior walked to their table and asked the waiter for two sandwiches to go. In the nearby street, cars were packed three deep, horns blared constantly and radios squalled. He gazed out over the bustling city and pictured it empty of people, the cars and trucks all stalled, not so much as a bird stirring. That was how it would look if the chemical weapon was employed.

Kuragin took her time. Bolan had eaten one of the sandwiches before she finally walked through the door and took a seat. "Anything?"

"No, but I am not surprised. If the traitor is here, he will keep a low profile."

"You told me at the château that one of the reasons you were picked for this job is because you know Dorsakov's habits. Be more specific. Does he have any special interests? Any hobbies? Anything that might help us track him down?"

"He likes soccer, which helps us very little because the odds of spotting him at a soccer match among thousands of people in the stands are very slim. He smokes a meerschaum pipe on occasion and is fond of Turkish tobacco."

"Does he womanize?" Bolan interrupted, and was given a look that would have withered a plant at ten feet. "What's the matter?"

"Nothing," Kuragin said testily. "No, he does not pursue loose women, if that is what you are asking. He is a traitor, not a lecherous pig. His social life has been limited since his wife died eight years ago. His children are all grown."

Bolan sat up. "He had a family? He gave me the impression he had been too wrapped up in his work to have one."

"Oh, he had one, all right. But he was also wrapped up in his job, as you put it. He was gone from home for days, sometimes weeks at a time. His wife hardly ever saw him, and his children could count on one hand the number of times he tucked them in at night. I am not surprised he gave you the impression he did. He was a terrible husband and worse father."

"You know an awful lot about his family life."

"The KGB kept track of its own."

Bolan had no doubt of that. He leaned back to stretch and relieve a cramp in his lower back. As he did, he gazed toward the street. To the south a driver was leaning on his horn with a heavy hand. Bolan idly turned to see why the driver was being so frantic and could hardly believe his eyes when the green four-door swerved onto the sidewalk and roared toward the café, scattering pedestrians and bicycle riders as if it were a huge bowling ball and they were so many bowling pins.

"It can't be!" Kuragin cried.

"It is," Bolan growled, jumping to his feet. He took only two steps toward their sedan when he realized they wouldn't reach it before the gunners reached the café. "Inside," he barked, and darted to the entrance.

For once Kuragin was slow. A submachine gun opened up, the barrel jutting from the passenger-side window of the green car. Slugs sliced into the patio around her feet, some chewing up a chair and table. Frantic patrons threw themselves to the ground, women screaming, several men cursing. She beat the lethal hail to the entrance by only a few steps.

Bolan seized her arm and yanked her in after him. Shifting, he shoved her to the floor and went prone on top of her as the glass door shattered under a barrage of 9 mm bullets. Then the magazine ran dry, and Bolan hauled her erect and ran toward a rear door. He was at a loss to understand how the gunners had found them so swiftly. But it was a problem better saved for later. At the moment he had to concentrate on staying alive.

The door opened onto an alley. People in the café were shouting, the owner bellowing like a bull, as Bolan slanted to the right. Trash cans lined the right-hand wall. Against the left-hand wall was a garbage Dumpster, its lid open. It gave him an idea.

Halting, the warrior grabbed the handles to one of the trash cans and moved it beside the bin. "You first," he said, offering his hand.

"What?" Kuragin glanced at the square mouth of the garbage container and was aghast. "Surely you don't want me to climb in *there?*"

"Would you rather be in a coffin?" Bolan gripped her by the waist and swung her onto the trash can. She gave him the sort of look a piranha might give its prey before it struck, but she obeyed and climbed inside. None too soon. Bolan heard the screech of tires near the end of the alley. He jumped onto the can, coiled his legs and leapt.

Kuragin was ankle deep in refuse, her nose scrunched up in distaste. Bolan landed beside her and drew the Desert Eagle this time. The growl of a car engine filled the alley, speeding toward them. There was the squeal of brakes, then a man's voice. The words were too low for him to hear, but he could tell the man wasn't speaking English. He straightened, his head rising above the rim of the garbage container, and began to bring up the big .44.

Suddenly Kuragin gave Bolan a sharp shove, knocking him against the side of the metal bin even as she raised her AutoMag.

The driver of the car was staring at the café. The second triggerman flung open the passenger door, jumped out and moved toward the café with a Czech Vz-58 braced against his side.

Neither man had a clue as to what hit them when the Russian agent cut loose. The Grizzly boomed twice. One shot drilled the head of the driver and slammed him onto the front seat. The other shot punched through the second gunner's spine between the shoulders blades and hurled him into the wall of the café. He slowly slumped, leaving a bright red smear in his wake.

Bolan heard sirens wail in the distance. He saw the green car start to creep forward as the dead driver's foot slipped from the brake pedal. Gripping the rim of the bin, he surged up and over, reaching the vehicle before it went ten feet. He wrenched the door open, jerked the driver out and slid behind the wheel. "Get in," he said harshly when he saw Kuragin clambering from the garbage container. Wearing a satisfied smirk, she ran around the car and slid inside.

Bolan floored the accelerator. At the end of the alley he took a left, and as he did a police car, sirens flashing, raced by, heading for the front of the café. Half a block later he turned right.

"Where are you going?" the Russian asked. "Our car is in the opposite direction."

"We'll use this one for a short while and then get another."

"But I left my overnight bag in the trunk. My change of clothes and personal items are in it. You have to go back so I can retrieve them."

Bolan shook his head. "Twice those guys found us even though we'd given them the slip. They must have had a means of tracking us. Maybe someone planted a bug in the sedan."

"How can that be? Your own people gave it to us at the airport. Wouldn't they have checked it out thoroughly first?"

"You'd think so," Bolan replied. "I don't have the answers yet." He jabbed a thumb at the glove compartment. "Check in there."

She did, but all she found was a map of the city, a map of the country and a risqué French magazine with a topless woman on the cover. "Decadent swine," she muttered, stuffing the magazine back.

The warrior had to confront the woman, but first they had to elude the Parisian police who would soon have a dragnet out for the green four-door.

A public parking lot appeared in the near distance. He pulled in, drove to the back row, and pulled into a slot. Before getting out he checked under the seat and discovered a manila folder. Opening it on his lap, he found himself staring at a black-and-white photograph of the woman next to him. Or, rather, half a photograph, for it clearly had been cut down the middle. She held someone's hand in hers, but the rest of the person had been chopped off at the wrist. Nothing else was in the folder.

Kuragin had opened her door and was about to step out. She glanced back, saw the photo and went rigid. "I do not believe it. Where could they have gotten that?"

"Your guess is as good as mine," Bolan replied. The photo appeared to have been taken quite a few years ago, judging by how young she looked. She had on a dress and high heels. "Do you remember when this was taken?"

"At a dance I attended before I joined the agency. I know, because I do not like having my picture taken and that is one of the few times it was done." She held out her hand. "May I?"

The warrior gave her the folder and climbed out. He locked all the doors, then opened the trunk. He didn't really expect to find anything but he did, a brown suitcase. The tabs popped right up when he flicked the release buttons.

"They came prepared, did they not?" Kuragin commented.

The suitcase contained an AKM with a folding stock, a 9 mm Beretta Model 12, a compact subgun with a wraparound bolt design similar to an Uzi's, and an M-63 machine pistol manufactured in Poland. The rest of the trunk was filled with magazines and boxes of ammo.

"Should we leave it here?"

"You never know when a little extra firepower might come in handy," Bolan said, taking out the suitcase and some of the ammo. He slammed the trunk lid and headed for a side street adjacent to the lot.

"Where do we go next?" the Russian inquired. "What is your plan?"

The truth was, Bolan didn't have one. Normally he tried to stay two steps ahead of the opposition, but so far the opposition had been three steps ahead of him. It had been that way ever since the mission started, when he walked into the trap set in the Black Forest by October Dawn. If he was the superstitious sort, which he wasn't, he'd be inclined to think the mission was jinxed.

The situation was made worse because the warrior had no idea whom he could trust. The business with the four gunners made him think they definitely had some way of keeping track of Kuragin and him. His experience with electronic surveillance equipment was limited, but he knew not to discount the possibility.

This wasn't the Executioner's usual quick in-and-out hard penetration of an enemy stronghold. He was more like a hunter this time around, stalking his prey in the midst of one of the most populated centers on the planet. And at the same time, he had enemies stalking him, enemies who were experts at the kind of cloak-and-dagger stuff he ordinarily shunned.

Whom could he trust? Bolan asked himself. With Able Team and Phoenix Force back in the States and none of the Stony Man crew on the mission, Brognola was the only one. Even the big Fed's people had to be suspect since any one of them might have gone sour if the price was right.

As for Marya Kuragin, she was a question mark. On the one hand Bolan felt an instinctive mistrust, partly due to her impetuous shooting back in the alley. On the other hand, the gunners had tried to nail her, too, which meant they weren't her own people.

Finally there was the Novichok-5 itself. A terrorist's dream weapon come true, it would draw every radical outfit in the Western Hemisphere like honey drew bears. If word leaked out that Dorsakov had gone into hiding in Paris, the City of Light would become a City of Death, a slaughter ground where rival factions fought with bloody abandon for the right to conduct mass genocide.

Bolan decided it was wisest to lie low for the time being. They would continue their search for Mikhail Dorsakov, but without the help of either Brognola's contacts or hers. He proposed the idea to her to test her reaction.

"I have no objections, Mr. Belasko," Kuragin said after a moment. "But our superiors will be greatly upset if we drop from sight. They are counting on us."

"But we can't count on them," Bolan stressed. "We're better off relying on our own resources. Brognola has worked with me long enough. He'll understand."

"I wish I could say the same about Valery Gorsky, the man I must answer to. He is a stickler for going by the book."

Bolan came to the street and headed east. "If we recover the Novichok-5, he'll forgive you."

"I would like to share your confidence, but I know him better than you."

Paris was a city famous for magnificent attractions such as the Eiffel Tower and its amazing architecture, but it was also a city notorious for its gruesome slums. And the slums were where Bolan was headed. No one would expect to find Kuragin and him there.

Bolan hailed a cab. Half an hour later he was setting the suitcase on a bed that sagged in the middle and had part of a spring sticking out of one side. He caught Kuragin's frown as he turned. "We're safe here," he said.

"Hardly. Did you see the way those shabby men in the lobby looked at me?" She wiped a finger on the lopsided dresser, smearing her fingertip with dirt. "It disgusts me to stay in a place like this, Mr. Belasko. You are asking a lot."

"We won't stay here any longer than we have to," Bolan assured her. He had asked the taxi to wait, so he hurried out and gave the driver the address for the third safehouse on the list. It turned out to be in the warehouse district bordering the Seine River. The sun was setting, and the surface of the wide river gave the illusion of being molten fire.

Most of the activity had stopped for the day. Businesses for the most part were closed or closing. Bolan had the driver go a block past the address and then stop. He was mildly surprised to learn the safehouse was a decrepit warehouse. As they drove by he saw a late-model car parked in front of the double doors. And briefly, through a grimy upstairs window, Bolan saw the outline of a moving figure.

Someone was there.

"How much longer are we going to wait?" Kuragin asked impatiently.

"Not much longer," Bolan replied. He had insisted on not making a move until the sun went down. They stood between two buildings within a stone's throw of the warehouse, watching the front entrance. No one had come or gone during the forty-five minutes they had been there.

The Russian agent had fidgeted nervously the whole time. Bolan had to put up with her pacing, tapping her feet and sighing once every minute. It made him wonder. She had been a model of self-control until they arrived at the warehouse. Why had she changed?

"Before we go in," the warrior said, "there's one thing we have to get straight."

Kuragin folded her arms and started to tap her foot again. "What is that?"

The warrior faced her. "I don't want you pulling another stunt like you did in the alley behind the café. I wanted to wound one of those men. We needed one alive so we could question him. But you blew both of them away before I had the chance."

"What did you expect?" the woman snapped. "They tried to kill me, remember?"

"They tried to kill both of us," Bolan reminded her. "People in our line of work can't afford to take things like that personally. It comes with the territory, Marya."

Kuragin held her head defiantly. "When someone tries to put a bullet into me, I take it very personally indeed. Anyone who says he doesn't is a liar."

Bolan refused to let her rile him. He lifted his chin at the warehouse and said calmly, "It might be Dorsakov in there. It might not. Whoever it is, he could have answers we need. So I want your word that you won't open up with that cannon of yours unless your life is in danger."

The agent's features clouded. "As I noted before, you ask a lot. I will not get myself killed because you are too soft for your own good."

So much for their personal détente, Bolan reflected. He would just have to keep an eye on her. Moving toward the warehouse, he kept one hand on the Beretta.

The double doors were big enough to admit big diesel rigs. Opening one was bound to make a lot of noise. Fortunately Bolan saw a smaller door at the corner and went to it. The knob turned smoothly.

As the warrior slipped inside he heard a loud crash from somewhere deep in the building. He drew up short, thinking their quarry was in the act of fleeing. Then an angry female voice rose to the rafters and was answered by a man. Another crash sounded. Bolan glanced at Kuragin, who arched her eyebrows while easing the door shut behind her.

A short corrugated hall brought them to a flight of metal steps that led to the upper level. Bolan started up first in a combat crouch, the Beretta clasped in a two-handed grip. A door to a large office stood open. The upper half of the office walls was tinted plastic. He scooted inside and stayed low so whoever else was in the warehouse wouldn't spot him.

The office was a shambles: the desk had been ransacked; a pair of file cabinets had been turned inside out; reams of loose and ripped papers covered the floor; the cushions to a small couch had been slashed to ribbons and the stuffing torn out.

Bolan moved to the left and rose high enough to see the warehouse proper. A man and a woman were conducting a search. They had already gone through a dozen crates and boxes, tearing them apart as they had torn apart the office. Both had black hair and wore black clothing, including black jackets with bulges that indicated the pair was armed.

The warrior turned to his companion to work out a course of action. Only she wasn't there. He sprinted to the top of the steps and saw her vanish among pallets piled high with goods. Holding a surge of anger in check, Bolan hastened after her. He couldn't let emotion cloud his judgment when that was all that stood between him and eternity.

The Executioner knew where she would go and went in the same direction. He prowled silently, glad the lighting was dim. The man and woman were still talking, in Arabic. The woman sounded angry; the man sounded bored.

Bolan finally drew close enough to see the pair. They were methodically searching through boxes of clothes. It didn't take a genius to figure out what they were after, nor to guess the organization to which they belonged.

Suddenly Marya Kuragin materialized beyond the pair, her Grizzly out and pointed at them. Bolan expected her to blast away but she advanced until she was right behind them, then shouted commands in their language. Both whirled, but neither was foolhardy enough to go for a weapon. Reluctantly they raised their arms.

Bolan stepped from concealment and covered them. "Nicely done," he said as he moved around in front of the pair.

"There are some things I know how to do right," Kuragin said, her voice betraying her resentment.

The raven-haired woman had volcanic eyes. "Who are you?" she demanded in English. "How dare you hold us at gunpoint!"

"How else should we hold two members of the Silver Crescent?" Bolan asked, stepping close enough to reach under her jacket and relieve her of a Sig-Sauer P-220. He backed up, set the weapon on a crate, then moved to her accomplice and palmed a Tanarmi .41 Action Express. It joined the P-220. "Now, suppose you tell us why you thought the Novichok-5 would be here?"

"I have no idea what you are talking about," the woman declared. "If you are officers of the law, we demand to see your identification."

"You are in no position to be making demands of anyone," Kuragin responded, taking a step closer. "I recognize this one from our files," she told Bolan. "Her name is Jafura Subay. She is second in command of their organization."

Subay showed her surprise. "My name is Nilifer. I do not know anyone named Subay," she claimed, her tone belying her statement.

The Russian took another step. "Where is Mikhail Dorsakov?"

"Who?"

"I warn you. You will tell me all you know, or you will suffer the consequences."

"I have never heard the name before," Subay said.

"Liar."

Bolan was keeping his eyes on the male terrorist. He intended to go to the office and phone Brognola so the big Fed could send in a retrieval team to spirit away the two fanatics. But the fierce twist of Kuragin's features made him hesitate. She had the air of a woman about to go over the edge, although why that should be, he couldn't guess.

"One last time," the Russian said. "Was Dorsakov here? Have you already disposed of him?"

"One last time," Subay mimicked her. "Who is this Dorsakov you keep mentioning? I do not know—"

The Silver Crescent terrorist got no further. With a savage lunge Marya Kuragin rammed the Grizzly into Subay's cheek, splitting the flesh and knocking the woman to the floor. "Did you kill him?" Kuragin raged, aiming at the terrorist's forehead.

Bolan edged toward her while keeping the Beretta on the man. "That's enough," he cautioned. "It's not our job to interrogate them. We'll leave that to those who do it best."

"Like hell we will," the Russian said. Snapping back her leg, she kicked Subay in the ribs. The Arab winced and bent at the waist, her face turning beet red.

"Did you kill Dorsakov?" Kuragin repeated. "I must know!"

"I would rather die!" Subay challenged her.

"Suit yourself."

Bolan tried to stop her, but Kuragin hauled off and planted her pointed shoe in Subay's ribs a second time.

The terrorist clasped her chest, writhing in agony. "I said that's enough and I meant it!" he said.

"Stay out of this," Kuragin rasped, motioning for him to stay back. "Dorsakov is ex-KGB. I have as much right to question her as anyone."

For a few moments the two of them were distracted, staring at each another and not the terrorists. It was a mistake the warrior would never make if he were by himself, and another sterling example of why he would rather work alone.

In those few moments, Jafura Subay exploded into action. She uncurled like a human whip and flipped a small, dark object at Bolan and Kuragin. In the same motion Subay rolled toward the nearest crates, while her companion threw himself backward.

Bolan was doing the same. For a few harrowing seconds he thought that Subay had hurled a grenade. In a sense, he was right, as he saw when white smoke spewed into the air. It was a smoke grenade.

The warrior pivoted and raised the Beretta to track the man, but a billowing cloud of smoke enveloped him. He could see no farther than the end of his nose. Almost at his elbow the Grizzly thundered, a waste of a round since he doubted Kuragin had hit anything. She was firing blind, another rank mistake. He slid to the left to get out of the cloud, careful not to collide with a pallet. Kuragin could have Subay. He would go after the companion.

Stepping into the clear, Bolan raced in the direction the man had gone, toward the rear of the warehouse. He caught sight of a dark head bobbing and weaving among the pallets. Pouring on the speed, he threaded a path through the crates. A door in the corner opened and banged shut. The Executioner knew the back of the building was right up against the Seine and wondered if the terrorist was going to try to swim to safety.

The warrior was ten feet from the door when the throb of a boat engine revealed that the terrorist had a better way to escape. He shoved on the door and saw the boat tied at the end of a short dock. Subay and her friend had to have arrived in it, not the car out front. Her companion was frantically trying to loosen the mooring line so he could flee.

Bolan had the fellow dead to rights. He charged, sighting down the 93-R. But the rope abruptly slipped free, the boat shot out from the dock and the man was spilled into the bottom of the craft. The Executioner had no target. He pumped his legs, reached the end of the dock as the boat began to gain speed of its own accord, and leapt with all his might, his arms and legs flailing as if he were trying to make a long jump. Which, in effect, he was. He crashed down into the boat, just as the terrorist started to rise.

The warrior tried to twist aside at the last moment but was unable to keep from slamming into his quarry. Both men lost their footing, Bolan falling atop the terrorist. He pressed the barrel of the Beretta against the man's side and clamped his finger on the trigger. But as he did, the boat gave a sharp lurch to starboard and the terrorist gave a convulsive heave. The Beretta slipped, just enough to spare the terrorist's life. The slug scored a furrow across his chest, inflicting a surface wound, no more.

It drove the hardman into a frenzy. He snatched hold of the warrior's wrist and tried to turn the 93-R toward Bolan. In the same breath he drove a knee at Bolan's groin to weaken him.

The Executioner shifted so that the knee hit his thigh, not his groin. Simultaneously he steeled his arm against the pressure being applied and arced his other elbow into the man's jaw. The terrorist weakened, though only for several seconds. Bolan tried to tear his arm free so he could use the Beretta, but the man clung to him for dear life.

Bolan struggled to his knees. He blocked a punch aimed at his face and countered with one to the solar plexus. Heaving upward, he nearly had his gun hand loose when the boat gave another lurch, throwing him against the side. The terrorist was thrown, too, his fingers biting into the warrior's wrist like claws.

For just a brief span Bolan saw the river. He realized the boat was heading for a high wall along the opposite shore. Unless it was brought under control quickly, they would crash.

The warrior hooked an ankle behind the terrorist and shoved. The man went down, still clinging to Bolan's wrist, still keeping the Beretta at bay. Lowering his left hand, Bolan drew the Desert Eagle in a cross draw, rammed the muzzle against the terrorist's chest and fired once.

The terrorist came up off the bottom as if trying to get airborne. His grip slackened and collapsed, his lips moving wordlessly as blood trickled from one corner. He clutched at Bolan once, then was still.

The Executioner had no time to spare. He leapt for the wheel. In front of him the flood wall loomed. The craft was so close that in another few heartbeats it would ram into the rampart. Bolan cut the wheel to the right and pushed on the throttle. Sloughing sideways, the boat created a wave that acted as a buffer, sparing the craft from damage by the width of a hand.

The warrior looped back into the Seine and cruised toward the warehouse. He was halfway across when he heard a pair of muted blasts. Opening the throttle all the way, he shot across to the dock and killed the engine so the craft drifted the final few feet.

Bolan vaulted from the boat and sped into the building. It was deathly quiet. He wanted to call Kuragin but dared not. By taking the rows between the pallets one at a time, he commenced a systematic search. It took a long time. Eventually, in a corner near the front door, he found the body.

Jafura Subay lay on her back, her arms outstretched, her eyes locked wide in the astonishment shared by many who died thinking they were invincible. She had been shot twice, once in the stomach, once in the right breast.

Now Bolan could call the Russian's name, and did so several times. There was no reply. He walked up to the ransacked office and gazed out over the warehouse. Kuragin was nowhere to be seen.

The warrior went outside and saw that the car that had been parked there was gone. Had the Russian taken it? Or, more importantly, if she had taken it, where had she gone? It made no sense to Bolan for her to have run out on him, not when she was under specific orders from the president of her country to help him track down the rogue.

Bolan set off at a jog toward a busy street in the distance. He came across a pay phone and hesitated. Touching base with Brognola might be a good idea. Within two minutes he had been patched through to the big Fed.

"How goes the war, Striker?"

"I feel like I'm running in circles. All three safehouses have been checked out but still no sign of Dorsakov."

"Damn. I hoped that idea would pan out."

"There's more," Bolan said, and told about the warehouse.

"I'll send in a retrieval team," Brognola said. "Anything else?"

"Our mutual friend has flown the coop."

"Were you behaving yourself?"

"Not funny," Bolan said, but grinned anyway.

"I'll get in touch with her side and have my own people investigate. You should think about getting some rest. If memory serves, you haven't slept in about forty hours. Where are you staying?"

Bolan gave him the name and address.

"All right. Call me back tomorrow morning, about eight. I might have something by then." Brognola paused. "One more thing. We have reason to believe the Red Dragons and the Burning Light have hit squads roaming the city looking for Mikhail Dorsakov. The way things are shaping up, you'll have to run a gauntlet of terrorists to get at him."

"All in a day's work," Bolan quipped. "Talk to you in the morning." He replaced the receiver and turned to go when a car honked at the nearby curb.

It was Marya Kuragin.

Bolan walked over and bent down. "Where the hell did you get to?"

"I was looking for you. I had heard a boat take off down the river and assumed you were on it. So I drove a few miles in both directions. When there was no trace of you, I decided I should go to our hotel and wait. I noticed you at this phone by accident."

The excuse was plausible but Bolan was skeptical. He went around to the passenger side and slid in. "The hotel it is, then, unless you'd like to grab a bite to eat first."

"That would be nice. And let us hope that this time we get to finish our meal in peace."

Bolan would rather have slept. He let her take him to a fancy restaurant not far off the Champs-Elysées. She was in surprisingly good spirits and smiled at him often. He ate light, but the Russian polished off an aperitif, hors d'oeuvres, a course of fresh fish, a course of meat and cheese and dessert. Then she ordered brandy.

"I hope you are not in any rush to get back to our pitiful excuse of a hotel," Kuragin said after taking a sip. "I do not want to spoil my mood."

"Is it Paris, or do you get off on blowing away terrorists?"

"That was crude, even for an American."

"You don't like Americans much, do you?"

"Normally I find them vain and boring," the woman said, leaning on her elbows. "You, however, are the exception to the rule. I cannot find a speck of vanity in you. Why is that? What makes you so different from the rest of your countrymen?"

"I'm not all that unusual. A lot of fine men and women put their lives on the line every day to safeguard our country."

"We both take our patriotism very seriously. Maybe we are more alike than you think." Her eyes narrowed, and the tip of her tongue traced the outline of her lower lip. "I find patriotic men extremely attractive. It is my one main weakness."

Bolan was mystified. He would never have expected her to come on to him, yet there she sat giving him the inviting look of a Parisian streetwalker.

"Do not look so puzzled," the woman said, reading his expression. "It is not often I meet a man like you." Her red lips curled. "Maybe you haven't noticed, Mr. Belasko, but I am a strong-willed woman. I have great strength of body and mind. And I like my men to be the same way. Sadly too few are."

"Where's a Samson when you need one?"

"A who?" Kuragin seemed perplexed, but only for a moment. "Oh. The biblical strongman. No, the strength I refer to must come from inside a man. You have that kind of strength. I can see it in your eyes, in the way you carry yourself."

Bolan simply stared. For her to give him two compliments in one minute was so out of character that he suspected she was up to something. All he said in response was "Thanks."

"I meant it," Kuragin insisted. "I suppose it comes from having had a strong father. He was made of iron, inside and out. And he tried to rear his children to be the same way. Anyone who showed weakness was punished severely. He kept a wide belt in the woodshed and was not against using it." She ordered more brandy.

"Shouldn't we be going?"

"What is your hurry? You told me that Mr. Brognola will not have any word for us until morning. Allow me my luxuries, if you do not mind."

Bolan sipped water until she had consumed several other drinks. She swayed as she stood, and leaned on him as he paid their bill. He put Kuragin on the passenger side and settled in the driver's seat. All he had to do to start the vehicle was touch the two wires together that she had stripped from the steering column when she stole the car. "We're getting rid of this first thing tomorrow," he said. "The last thing we need is to be picked up by the Paris police in a hot car."

"Hot?"

"As in stolen."

"You worry too much," Kuragin said, and giggled.

Bolan stuck to the speed limit so as not to attract unwanted attention. His partner tried to stay awake, but her eyes kept closing and her chin drooped to her chest. Soon she rested her head on the back of the seat and curled her body so her back was to the door. "Hold on," he said. "We'll be at the hotel in a few minutes. You can have the bed."

"If you think I am going to sleep in that filthy hovel, you are mistaken."

"Do you have somewhere else to spend the night?"

"Right here."

"It's too risky," Bolan said.

"No riskier than sleeping in that miserable bed," Kuragin retorted sluggishly. "It probably has lice. So no thanks. You can have it if you want. I'm not budging. I'll lock the doors and lie on this seat. No one will even know I'm in here."

Bolan tried to talk her out of it but she had made up her mind. She fell asleep long before they reached the slum. He parked under a tree across the street from their hotel, eased her onto her side and got out. He verified all the doors were locked, then went into the lobby. The desk clerk was too busy reading a girlie magazine to even look up.

Bolan walked past the stairs that would have taken him to his room. He turned into a short hall, which brought him to an exit door at the side of the building.

It creaked as he stepped out into an alley so choked with refuse the stench was awful. Staying as close to the wall as he could, he ventured near enough to the street to see the car.

He didn't have long to wait. A minute later Kuragin's head popped up. She glanced at the hotel, then flicked the headlights on and off twice.

A block away someone in another parked car answered in kind. The engine turned over, and the vehicle slowly drove toward the hotel.

Bolan placed a hand on the Desert Eagle. He figured that the newcomers were coming for him, and he would rather confront them outside where he had room to move and no civilians were in jeopardy.

The second car braked in front of the hotel. Two men were in the front seat. The driver got out.

The warrior drew the Desert Eagle.

Unexpectedly the driver opened the back door and climbed back in. Kuragin slid from her vehicle, dashed across the street with one eye on the windows above and got behind the wheel. She said something that made the two men laugh. Punching the gas pedal, she drove off.

Bolan let them travel a few blocks before he ran to the stolen car, started it and made a sharp U-turn. Kuragin and her friends were almost out of sight. He accelerated until he was at an ideal tailing distance and maintained it. The idea occurred to him that they might know he was following, that they might be leading him into a trap. It didn't matter.

One way or the other the warrior was going to find out what the Russian Intelligence agent was up to.

11

Two hours later the Executioner pulled off a narrow country road onto the shoulder. Ahead of him rose a steep hill. Kuragin's car had turned off onto a gravel drive that curved to the crest, where a large country house sat silhouetted against the backdrop of stars. Several lights were on.

Bolan left his vehicle and entered the dank woods. After almost two full days without sleep he could feel fatigue gnawing at him, but he shook it off. By sticking to open ground he made good headway until he came to the base of the slope. There was cover but not much. He had to climb using his hands and knees. It was slow going, more so near the top when he found that erosion had worn the topsoil away leaving loose earth that rattled out from under him and made it hard for him to get purchase.

All the while the warrior had to train one eye on the house. There was a possibility they had motion or infrared sensors installed. He'd be a sitting duck if they detected him before he reached the top. Clinging to the slope as he was, he wouldn't even be able to draw a pistol.

At length Bolan neared the crest and the ground leveled off. He crept to a row of shrubbery and followed it until he was near the corner of the house. In addition to the car driven by Kuragin, a compact model sat in the driveway.

Bolan paused and gazed toward Paris. The hill was so high he could see for miles. An endless carpet of forest and rolling hills broken by random patterns of village lights and a few towns stretched to the horizon. A set of headlights was visible a few miles away.

The warrior crept along the wall to the back of the house until he reached a door. He tried the knob, which turned easily. Holding the silenced Beretta next to his ear, Bolan crossed the threshold and started down a short hall toward the sound of voices. Several people were conversing in Russian.

He stopped at the end of the hall and peered around the corner into a spacious living room. Four people were present. Marya Kuragin sat on a sofa, gesturing angrily at a bald man in a chair. Two younger men stood on either side of a cold fireplace. All four held drinks, not guns.

Two swift strides took the warrior into the room. "Nobody move," he commanded in Russian, the Beretta trained on Kuragin.

The woman was the only one who didn't seem shocked by the warrior's sudden advent. She merely blinked a few times. "Mr. Belasko," she said, "you are more resourceful than I gave you credit for being. How did you know I would sneak off on you?"

"It was all those compliments," Bolan replied, stepping to the right so he could put his back to the wall. The bald man was taking his arrival calmly enough, but the two by the fireplace had the edgy look of men who sorely wanted to go for their hardware. "I don't think your friends there care whether you get shot," he commented.

Kuragin spoke sharply to the two in Russian, and they looked properly cowed. "They are recent recruits," she told the warrior. "And you know how impetuous novices can be."

"Government agents?" Bolan said, nodding at all three.

"Yes."

He nodded. "So let me hear what this is all about, partner. And make it good."

"I do not have to make it anything. The truth will be enough," Kuragin stated. She set her glass on a table and leaned back. "Under orders from my government, I have been holding a few things back from you."

"Am I supposed to be surprised?" Bolan said dryly.

The woman ignored him. "Paris, as you well know, is the gateway to Europe. It has long been a hub of spy activity, a shuttle point, if you will, for agents traveling in both directions. We maintain a number of houses for their use."

"And this is one," Bolan deduced.

"It is. Until a few months ago it was in almost constant use. It is as likely a place as any for the traitor to hide out in."

"So you took it on yourself to come see without confiding in me. That was why you pretended to be so tired that you couldn't hold your head up. You wanted to be left in the car so you could slip off without my noticing."

"I should have known better," Kuragin said. She glanced at the Beretta. "Now that you know, there is no need for the pistol. We are still on the same side, temporarily at least, and you have nothing to fear from us."

Bolan made no move to lower the 93-R. "Where did you disappear to at the warehouse?"

"To phone in for instructions. Just as you have been doing. I did not think I would be gone that long." Kuragin crossed her legs. "My contact gave me this address, and I was instructed to check it out at the first opportunity."

"Have you found anything?"

"The renegade was here but he is gone. I found an empty pouch of pipe tobacco in a trash can, the brand he always uses. It is my guess that he stayed here for a short while weeks ago, well before the debacle at the château."

Bolan recalled the visit Dorsakov had made to Paris to recruit the street toughs. "What's your next step?"

"I planned to drive back into the city and spend the rest of the night in the car. In the morning when you came out, you would have been none the wiser." She sighed. "Now we might as well spend the night here. There are plenty of bedrooms. And no lice."

The idea of sleeping in the same house as four Russian agents hardly appealed to Bolan. There had been a time when they would have given anything for his head on a platter, and old hatreds died hard. "I'll take a page from your book and sleep in the car."

"Whatever for?" Kuragin asked. "Don't you like our company?"

Bolan was spared from having to answer by a sudden loud buzzing that emanated from another room. He cocked his head at the woman. "Is someone else here?"

"It's the motion alarm at the end of the driveway," the woman replied, appearing puzzled.

"Are you expecting company?"

"No, but it has to be some of our people. No one else knows about this place." She paused. "Or perhaps it is just someone who pulled into the drive to turn around. It happens every now and then."

The buzzing stopped abruptly.

"There is a second sensor a few hundred feet from the road. If that one goes off, then we definitely do, as you put it, have company."

They all sat in tense silence for not quite ten seconds. Then the second alarm went off, a thin but high-pitched beeping.

"They are coming to the house," Kuragin stated, and straightened as an idea struck her. "What if it is the traitor?"

The warrior couldn't see the wily Dorsakov being stupid enough to return to a hideout already abandoned, but he had to admit there was a slender possibility.

Kuragin rose. "It's too late to turn out the lights. They can be seen from a long way off. The best we can do is hide." She started to reach under her jacket for the Grizzly but stopped and glanced at Bolan. "With your permission, of course."

The buzzer alarm went off again and buzzed longer this time, which indicated the object that triggered the sensor had taken its sweet time going past.

"There are two cars," Kuragin said, worry lines creasing her brow. The other agents appeared equally ill at ease. "I do not know what to make of it. This is very strange."

"I suggest we be ready for anything," Bolan said.

Nodding, Kuragin gave terse orders in Russian. The bald man and the young agents left the room and turned left down another hallway. She fell into step behind them. Bolan walked well to the rear so he could keep an eye on everyone.

They came within sight of the front door. Kuragin and the bald man stepped into doorways on either side of the hall. At a sharp word from her, the two younger men drew 9 mm Makarov pistols and advanced slowly.

Everyone heard the crunch of tires on gravel. A car door slammed, then another. A loud voice could be heard, coming closer. The language being spoken was Russian. Seconds later someone pounded on the door and a man called out, "Open the door, Comrades. We have a message to deliver."

Kuragin and her companions relaxed. The two young men lowered their Makarovs and one of them stepped to the door and opened it, his face lighted by a smile of greeting.

Bolan had hung back far enough to cover all of them in case it was an elaborate trick. The young agents blocked his view of whoever stood on the steps, so the first inkling he had that the new arrivals weren't really Russians was when a subgun chattered and the agent who had answered the knock was drilled with holes. As the man buckled, Bolan saw the shooter, Japanese by the looks of him, wielding an M-3 A-1 grease gun. The second young Russian whipped up his Makarov, but he was too slow. A row of slugs from the grease gun dropped him to the floor.

Bolan dived into a room as Marya Kuragin and the bald Russian opened fire with their pistols. The gunner on the porch darted to the right. They missed him but splintered the jamb.

The second young agent was still alive, moaning and writhing feebly in acute torment.

Kuragin looked at the man and went to take a step toward him when the entrance was filled by another Japanese gunner. This one held a 9 mm Gustav M-45 B submachine gun with a 40-round magazine. He snapped a few shots at her, but she ducked into the room. Pivoting, the shooter sent a few rounds at the bald Russian. Then, grinning wickedly, he drilled the groaning agent in the forehead.

Bolan, so far, had been overlooked. As he took aim at the Japanese, he had an intense feeling of being watched. Sinking into a crouch, the Executioner swiveled and saw a third gunner who had been about to plug him in the back. This one had a MAC-10. The shooter squeezed the trigger, rushing his shots, the burst peppering the door inches above Bolan's head. The warrior got off a single round, the 9 mm Parabellum bullet penetrating the bridge of the gunner's nose and blowing out the back of his head.

Bolan's educated guess was that the attackers were members of the Red Dragons. How the Japanese had found the safehouse was anyone's guess. At the moment, he had more important things to worry about, such as getting out alive. The gunners on the porch were keeping Kuragin and the bald agent pinned down. Unless he bailed them out, they would eventually run out of ammo and be picked off.

The warrior shoved the 93-R into its rig, crouched and leapt. He reached the dead terrorist's side and scooped up the MAC-10. Whirling, he fired at the gunner with the grease gun, who jerked back from sight. "Come on!" he shouted at Kuragin. "I'll cover you!" He drilled more rounds into the doorjamb to deter the Japanese.

Kuragin and the bald agent were quick to take advantage. Adding the firepower from their pistols to the din, they retreated toward the warrior, each hugging a wall so he would have a clear line of fire. All three of them gained the safety of a bend in the hall, and halted.

"I can't believe this!" the woman declared. "Who are they? Why are they after us?"

"They're Red Dragons," Bolan said, and used the last of the ammo in the MAC-10. "They want to get their hands on Dorsakov, not us. We just happened to be here."

"How many do you think there are?"

"Two carloads," Bolan reminded her. He tossed away the MAC-10 and unleathered the Desert Eagle.

Kuragin cursed in Russian as she fed a new magazine into her Grizzly.

"They have us outgunned and outnumbered," the warrior said. "Do you have any heavy artillery stashed somewhere?"

"Just what we have on us."

It figured, Bolan thought. He remembered the breaking glass and shifted so he could watch the corridor behind them. "We have to get out of here," he stated quietly so the Japanese wouldn't overhear. The firing had stopped, but he knew the terrorists were still out there, maybe fanning out to surround the house if they hadn't done so already.

"There is the back door," Kuragin whispered.

"These guys are pros. They'll be watching it. Let's try an upstairs window. It's the one thing they might not anticipate."

"Follow me," the woman said, and turned.

Beyond her a shadow materialized from out of a room. In pure reflex Bolan fired the Desert Eagle twice, and the gunner oozed to the floor. The Executioner and the bald Russian dogged her heels to a flight of stairs. They passed the dead Japanese, and Bolan helped himself to the man's mini-Uzi. He dallied long enough to pat the terrorist's pockets. The search yielded three spare magazines.

From outside came loud whispers and furtive movements. Bolan was last up the steps. They went into the first room, a bedroom, and moved to a window on the side of the house that overlooked the steep drop-off.

Kuragin undid the latch, took hold of the sash bars and eased the window upward, pausing whenever the window squeaked. Soon she had it high enough.

Bolan stepped to one side of the window and peeked out. There was no sign of anyone below, but he knew all too well how deceiving appearances could be. A gunner might be just around the corner, watching. "I'll go first," he volunteered. He slipped a leg out, then the other, and eased his torso through. For a moment he sat balanced on the sill. Then he shoved off, using the soles of his feet, and fell twelve feet to the grass. Landing lightly, the warrior braced his back against the wall and looked to the right and left, expecting gunners to appear. None did.

He moved aside and motioned. The bald Russian was next and he landed badly, thudding against the house. Both of them froze, but there were no outcries. Seconds later Kuragin joined them, landing like a cat.

Bolan headed toward the corner nearest the driveway. He saw three cars, not four, and wondered where the other vehicle had gotten to. From inside the house came a low thump. Tapping Kuragin and the other agent, he pointed at the drop-off. It was the quickest way down off the hill, and once they reached the forest they would be relatively safe.

Kuragin nodded curtly.

Crouching, the warrior sprinted along the shrubbery. It ended short of the edge, but he kept on going. Speed was essential now. They had to climb down before they were spotted.

It was too late. A strident shout pierced the darkness, and a subgun opened up from inside the front hall.

Rounds bit into the ground all around Bolan as he spun, hefted the Uzi and replied in kind. It was too dark to tell if he scored or not, but the subgun did cease firing. "Move it!" he directed, and gave Kuragin a shove. She twisted and snaked over the edge. The bald man stepped forward to do the same.

An upstairs window exploded in a shower of glass, and a Red Dragons terrorist brought a submachine gun to bear. Slugs ripped a path across the lawn, through the shrubbery and into the back of the bald Russian. He grunted with the impact, threw his arms out, then pitched over the rim.

There was a thud, and Kuragin cried out.

Bolan dropped onto all fours. He saw the two agents tumbling groundward, the bald one limp and lifeless, Kuragin struggling to untangle her legs from his. Without hesitation he threw himself down the slope, twisting so he slid on his backside. Above him the ground erupted in geysers as the Red Dragons hardman opened up again.

The warrior gained speed swiftly. When he reached the incline below the drop-off, he shot across it toward a cluster of trees. Slamming into them at that speed would break both his legs. He tensed his stomach muscles, held the Uzi to his chest so he wouldn't lose his grip and threw himself to the right.

Bolan swerved past the tree trunks, but his lunge sent him rolling out of control. He hit a brush and winced as its thin branches gouged his ribs. Then he hit a bump, flew a few feet and smacked into a log. For a few dazed moments he lay on his back, collecting his breath. Then he pushed up off the grass and scoured the area for Kuragin. She had to be somewhere nearby, but he couldn't spot her. Then he spied the outline of a body. It was the bald Russian, not Kuragin, lying facedown.

A twig snapped in the woods. Bolan realized Kuragin was fleeing and headed after her. Behind him several figures were converging. The Red Dragons opened up as he plunged into the pines. Bullets clipped branches and pine cones on either side. Several whizzed past so close he could have sworn they fanned his hair. He caught no glimpse of the Russian woman even though he pushed himself to his utmost.

In all the excitement Bolan had lost his bearings. But a single look at the sky was all it took to get a fix. By the position of the North Star he learned that he was heading north, as Kuragin had been, when he should be heading to the south to return to the car. He angled to the right a few feet, where the ground was more open, hoping to see Kuragin. All he did was draw the fire of the gunners.

The warrior drew up in the shelter of a wide trunk. Only one of the Red Dragons was in sight. Raising the Uzi, he led the running form by a quarter of an inch, then applied his finger to the trigger. The man silently dropped to the ground.

Bolan broke from the trunk and sprinted off. It would have been smart of Kuragin to wait for him so they could fight together. The fact she hadn't made him wonder if she was trying to give him the slip again.

The trees thinned, ending at a meadow. Bolan stopped, unwilling to expose himself. He jogged to the left with the intention of skirting the meadow but stopped short when, several hundred feet to the east, the forest echoed to sustained gunfire. Subguns rattled, pistols cracked. He knew it had to be Kuragin and ran to her aid.

As long as the firing continued, Bolan had no difficulty homing in on the firefight. But he wasn't quite halfway there when the shooting ended. He paused to listen and heard only the wind.

The warrior went on carefully, stopping frequently to scour the terrain ahead. Eventually he saw a body. Slinking through the grass, he crept close enough to determine it was the body of a terrorist, not the agent.

Bolan started a sweep of the area. He hunted for minutes and was about ready to concede he was wasting his time when the wind brought him the sound of a car starting, up at the house. Either the Red Dragons were leaving or Kuragin had given them the slip and was escaping. He ran toward the hill. Taillights receded along the gravel drive.

The bald Russian lay on his side instead of facedown. As Bolan went by him, the man groaned. The Executioner stopped and squatted. He touched the man's shoulder and the Russian's eyes snapped wide. They wouldn't stay open long. The agent had so many holes in him, it was a wonder he had lived as long as he had.

"Save her," the man croaked in poor English.

"Marya?"

"Bastards got her. Saw them drag her off."

"I'll do what I can."

The Russian sucked in a breath and gripped the warrior with the last of his fading strength. "You must. She is important. She is—" The man gurgled deep in his throat and trembled for a few seconds. Somehow, he managed to rasp out the rest. "She is Dorsakov's daughter."

With that, he died.

12

The rap of a fist on the door of Mack Bolan's room woke him from a sound sleep several hours later. "Yes?" he called out.

"Telephone, sir."

"Thanks," Bolan said, and slid from the bed. He stretched, donned his jacket and went out. The phone was an old rotary instrument at one end of the front desk. He tucked the receiver to his ear and turned his back to the desk clerk, a portly man whose hairy belly stuck out from under a grimy shirt. "Belasko."

"Sorry to ruin your beauty sleep, Striker," Hal Brognola said, "but we have a hot lead. You need to act right away."

"How hot?"

"I pulled a few strings. Bouvier, the French liaison, got in touch with the chief of the Paris police. It turns out they've had their eye on a certain Japanese importer named Ikano who has a loft on the Right Bank. He's suspected of funneling money to the Red Dragons. If they're lying low, that's where they'll be."

"I can be there within the hour," Bolan said, "but I don't want interference. Do the police have it under surveillance?"

"They've pulled their men out of deference to us. We have a free hand."

"Anything new on the daughter's background?"

"I made an official request through channels, but the Russians have yet to reply to my request for confirmation. Just between you and me, I think we threw them for a loop on this one. They never figured we'd learn the truth." Brognola paused. "Do you still stand by your source?"

"The man was dying. He had no reason to lie," Bolan said. "The end of the cold war hasn't changed the Russians one bit. It's just like them to send a woman to kill her own father."

"Maybe they figured she's the only one who can get close to Dorsakov without him unleashing the Novichok-5."

"Has there been anything new on him?"

"No. He's still in hiding. I'd be willing to bet he hasn't slipped through the net we've thrown around Paris. But we can't keep the whole country on alert forever. He can wait us out. Then when things are back to normal, he'll be free to set up another auction. We'll be back to square one."

"Keep me posted. I'm on my way to the loft."

"Hold up a minute. I'm not done yet," Brognola said. "I took the liberty of having a car delivered out front while you slept. A brown Mercedes."

"I didn't want anyone else but you to know where I'm staying," Bolan said pointedly.

"If you still think there's a traitor at my end, you can forget it. Those four who tailed you from Orly were Russian Intelligence."

Bolan was surprised. It made no sense for the Russian to try to kill him when he was working with the unofficial sanction of the highest echelons of their government. And it made even less sense for them to try to kill Marya Kuragin, or whatever her true name might be, since she was one of their own. "It doesn't add up," he remarked.

"Not yet. But I have people working on it. Eventually we'll uncover their motive. I hate to see you run this gauntlet alone. Maybe I should send in Phoenix Force to back you up."

"No. By the time they got here, it might all be over. Hold them in reserve in case something happens to me. I've gone this far by myself. I'll go the distance."

"Take care, then."

The dial tone sounded in Bolan's ear, and he set down the phone. In under two minutes he went back upstairs for the brown suitcase he had taken from the trunk of the Russian agents' car and hurried out to the Mercedes. The key was taped to the upper side of the visor.

It was a long drive to the Right Bank. Here stood many of the city's most famous landmarks. He wrestled with the heavy traffic in the Place de la Concorde, drove past the Grand Palais, and was soon among tightly packed stone buildings built a century ago. The address he wanted was on a side street. He parked a block away, pulled up his collar, and strolled up the street.

All the curtains in the loft had been closed, which Bolan took as a good sign. There was no fire escape, though, which was bad. The bottom floor was taken up by a bakery. Bolan glanced in through the window and saw a stocky Frenchman selling fresh bread to an elderly woman. Several girls were examining pastries. He ducked into the first alley he came to and worked around behind the building. The rear door was securely locked.

Stymied, Bolan returned to the car. He faced a no-win situation. If he went busting into the loft, the baker and his customers were in danger of taking a few stray rounds. Yet he couldn't just sit there and wait for the bakery to close. There was no telling what the Red Dragons were doing to Kuragin.

He'd have to try a quiet approach. Opening the suitcase, he removed the M-63 machine pistol and several spare magazines. Then he slipped his right arm out of the coat and folded the sleeve to give the impression he lacked the limb.

Glancing around to be certain no pedestrians were watching, Bolan lowered the front grip on the M-63 until it locked at a ninety-degree angle. He retracted the butt and turned it into position. In effect he had transformed the pistol into a very compact subgun.

Stuffing the 25-round magazines in his pockets, Bolan held the M-63 under his coat, the bolt open, and slid from the vehicle. A gust of wind nearly tore the coat from his right shoulder, but he caught it with his left hand and pulled it close around him.

The bakery shop was empty except for the baker, who stared idly at the sparse traffic. Bolan nodded and went in through the door to the left of the shop's. A high flight of stairs led to the loft. He'd climbed only six of them when the door behind him opened.

The big man spun, his finger on the trigger of the machine pistol. In the nick of time he saw it was the baker, not one of the Japanese. The baker offered a friendly smile and spoke in rapid-fire French.

"I'm sorry," Bolan said when the Frenchman took a breath, "but my French is very rusty. Do you speak English?"

"*Oui.* A little," the baker said. He indicated the loft. "Mr. Ikano not here. Go maybe an hour ago. Him, and all his friends."

"Was there a woman with them?"

"Yes. Very *jolie,* that one. Very pretty."

Bolan frowned. He was too late. The Red Dragons had flown the coop and taken Kuragin with them.

The baker saw the frown and his own smile widened. "Not worry, eh? Monsieur Ikano come my place. Buy pastry. Say he go to business. You understand? *Comprenez-vous?*"

"Yes," Bolan assured him. "Thank you very much." He hastened to the car and went in search of a phone. It took a while to get through to Brognola.

"Striker, do you have her already?"

"I wish. I need the address of Ikano's import business. For some reason they took her there."

"Give me a minute."

In half that time Brognola was back on the line and gave the warrior the address. He also had new information to impart. "I've received word that the Russian Intelligence is having a fit over Kuragin's abduction. Sources tell me that they've sent in two or three teams to find her, against all protocol. And given that they've tried to rub you out once already—"

"Odds are they'll try again if I cross their path," Bolan finished for him. It wasn't bad enough he had to contend with Dorsakov and the various terrorist factions who wanted to get their hands on the Novichok-5. He also had to be on his guard against the agency his so-called partner belonged to.

"It's turning into a shooting gallery, Striker," Brognola said, "and you're one of the clay targets. I know you won't let me call in Phoenix Force, but how about if I send over a couple of my most reliable men? Just to back you up in case push comes to shove."

"You know better. Talk to you later."

Toshiro Ikano's import business was located within two blocks of the Seine in a business district. It was a newer building, set off by itself at one end of a large lot. The parking area was full of employee cars, it being a weekday. Bolan went around the block, studying the layout. There were two doors into the building, one on the north side, the other on the south, with receptionists at each. Gaining entry without being spotted would be impossible.

A third door earned Bolan's attention. This one was an exit on the west side. He parked and walked up to it as if he had every right to be there. A single jerk of the knob confirmed the door was locked.

The smart thing to do, Bolan reflected, would be to wait until quitting time when all the employees went home. But by then Dorsakov's daughter might be dead. So with his coat arranged to give the impression he only had one arm and the machine pistol snug against his leg, Bolan entered Ikano Imports on the north side and gave his most charming smile to the buxom secretary. "Mike Belasko. I have an appointment to see Mr. Ikano."

The secretary consulted her appointment book, then looked up, puzzled. "I am so sorry, *monsieur.* It is not listed. Perhaps you have the wrong day, *non?*"

"No," Bolan assured her. "It was set up weeks ago. I don't understand why you have no record of it." He tapped her intercom. "Why don't you give Mr. Ikano a buzz and ask if he'll see me anyway? I'm sure he will. Tell him it's about the package from Russia he picked up last night."

"I don't know," the secretary said. "Monsieur Ikano left instructions that he was not to be disturbed under any circumstances."

"Call him," Bolan urged. "He won't hold it against you. I promise."

Appearing as if she would rather walk barefoot across broken glass, the secretary did as the warrior wanted. She flashed her white teeth when she hung up. "You were right. He will see you. Please take the elevator on the right to the second floor. His security people will meet you and escort you to his office."

"Security?"

"*Oui.* Mr. Ikano imports state-of-the-art, high-tech electronic equipment from his country," the secretary said, sounding as if she were quoting a promotional brochure. "Everything from video records to hardware with military applications. One of his clients is the French army. So naturally he is quite security conscious."

"Naturally."

"Why, in three short years he's built up this business from nothing to a multimillion-franc enterprise," the secretary boasted as if she were the CEO. "It's the wave of the future, you see."

"What is?"

"Japanese products. One day they'll have a monopoly worldwide, if you ask me. I—"

"Thank you," Bolan cut her off. "I had better go. Wouldn't want to keep your boss waiting, would we?"

The warrior walked to the elevator and pressed the button for the second floor. No sooner did the doors close than he drew the Beretta 93-R and crouched against the wall below the control panel. He expected to be greeted by Frenchmen in security guard uniforms when the car stopped and the doors hissed open. Instead, a pair of Japanese in suits were waiting, and each had a hand under his jacket. They took one look and tried to draw their hardware.

The cough of the suppressor was no louder than a man's cough would be as Bolan drilled both men through the head. He stepped into a plush hallway and scanned for other security personnel, but there was none.

The warrior paused long enough to rip open the shirt on one of those he had slain. Staring up at him was the distinctive chest tattoo that gave the Red Dragons their name. He ran to the door at the end of the corridor, which opened at the slightest touch into an anteroom filled with chairs. Beyond was a door cracked open a hair. He pushed ever so gently and entered a spacious office, the 93-R in one hand, the machine pistol in the other.

The head of the company sat at a wide mahogany desk. He had his back to the door and was speaking in Japanese into a phone. After a few moments he said, *"Sayonara,"* and hung up. An expression of shock covered his face when he swiveled his chair. But he recovered quickly and declared in English, "You are bold, American. I will grant you that, even if I cannot credit you with much intelligence in coming here after her."

"You know who I am?" Bolan said, walking to the right so he could see if Ikano made a stab at a drawer or a button.

"We are not without our sources, Belasko. We knew she was working with an American, and my men caught a glimpse of you at the safehouse last night. A pity they didn't finish you off as they did the Russian vermin."

Two particular words rang in Bolan's mind like the peeling of a bell. "Your men?" he emphasized. "That would make you the head of the Red Dragons."

Ikano didn't respond. He didn't have to. His face answered for him.

"And here everyone thinks you're just their money man," Bolan said, halting. He was impressed by the clever scheme. It explained why the Japanese authorities hadn't been able to put a crimp in the Red Dragons' activities for so long. They would never have suspected a prosperous businessman of being the leader. Only recently had Ikano come under scrutiny, and then only at the financial end. "Wait until I pass on the word."

"You will not live long enough to tell anyone," Ikano said. "My advice to you is to turn around and leave while you still can. What is this woman to you, anyway?"

"I could ask you the same thing about the Dragons," Bolan replied. "Why would a man who has everything to live for risk losing it all by setting up an organization of fanatics?"

"To recapture a dream, Mr. Belasko," Ikano said. "Japan will never attain her proper place as the greatest nation on this globe until she rebuilds her military might. And as long as Washington's puppets are in power in my country, that will never be. I have pledged myself to using every means at my disposal to bring the government down, to make the people see the truth."

Bolan thought it strange that the fanatical rightwinger saw fit to confide in him. Then his internal alarm went off. The man wasn't confiding. Ikano was stalling, or maybe trying to keep him distracted long enough for—what?

The warrior crouched and spun, and saw a hardman by the door, a pistol raised to fire. He shot first. The slug slammed the man against the wall. Bolan pivoted to cover Ikano before the businessman got any ideas, but Ikano was one step ahead of him. Literally.

Ikano had risen and was dashing toward a recessed doorway at the other end of the room. He looked back and sneered, perhaps because he mistook Bolan for a typical government agent, and typical government agents never shot unarmed suspects in the back. He was thinking that he would make it through the door and escape. But he was wrong on both counts. There was nothing typical about the Executioner. And the businessman never reached the door.

The warrior squeezed the Beretta's trigger twice. Ikano was flung forward by the heavy impact of the Parabellum manglers and landed on his stomach, his head twisted to one side, an expression of disbelief etched on his features.

Bolan holstered the 93-R and walked to the door. A short flight of stairs angled to the third floor. He started up, pausing between each step, his senses primed. Yet another door appeared on the right. From within came voices talking in Japanese.

Crouching, the Executioner rotated the knob, ever so slowly. He put his eye to the crack and saw a wide room, one side piled high with boxes. On the other side sat a single wooden chair. Tied to it, bound hand and foot, was Marya Dorsakov. She had been stripped naked, and her body bore a dozen nasty bruises and welts.

Five Red Dragons terrorists were enjoying themselves. Four ringed the chair, either standing or seated on boxes. The fifth man held a metal baton that he was smacking against the palm of his own hand. He had an air of latent cruelty about him that no expensive business suit and neatly trimmed hair could dispel.

As Bolan watched, the interrogator faced the Russian and planted his feet.

"How much longer will you be stubborn, woman?" the man said in precise English. "You have suffered a great deal, and for nothing. We will get the information out of you in time."

Kuragin's head hung low. Blood trickled from a corner of her split lower lip as she raised her head and regarded her tormentor defiantly. "I have already given you the only answer I can. I do not know where the traitor is. I do not know where you can find the Novichok-5."

The interrogator suddenly lashed out, driving the end of the baton into the pit of Kuragin's stomach. She cried out, then sagged, her abdomen quivering.

"I have gone easy on you so far, woman," the man snarled. "But my patience is at an end. Ikano-san expects results. If you do not tell us, I will start removing parts of your body you can do without. I will start with your fingers, then cut off your toes. If you still refuse to tell us, you will be skinned alive."

One of the other Dragons snickered.

"You can scream all you want," the interrogator went on. "These walls are soundproofed, so no one will hear. And do not expect your compatriots to come to your rescue. They have no idea where to find you."

Kuragin raised her head and glared. "You are fools."

"Oh? Ikano-san was smart enough to have us keep an eye on the Russian embassy. And when we saw several carloads of new arrivals, it was not hard to figure out that they were agents sent to find your traitor. We tailed them when they separated. It is true that some of them gave us the slip, but the bald one led us to the house on the hill. We hoped that Dorsakov would be there. It was most unfortunate he was not. But we did take you alive, so our effort wasn't wasted." He smiled smugly. "For the last time, where do your people think he is hiding?"

"We have no idea."

The torturer sighed and motioned. One of the others reached under his jacket and produced a tanto, a short sword, fifteen inches in length, which was exchanged for the baton. The one with the cruel features slipped the tanto from its sheath and held the blade close to Kuragin's face. "This is razor sharp. It will take off your fingers as easily as if I were cutting paper."

Kuragin straightened and held her chin defiantly. "Do what you will. I have nothing more to say to you."

Extending the sword, the torturer took hold of the first finger on her right hand. "It matters not to me, woman. If you don't tell us, we will find another Russian to question. Sooner or later we will learn what we need to know."

The warrior had heard enough. Holding the machine pistol in both hands, he eased the door outward and slipped in with his back to the wall. The Dragons were so intent on the torture about to unfold that none looked in his direction. He took a few more steps to give himself a better angle.

It was then that one of the terrorists glanced around, blinked in surprise and shouted a warning.

Bolan fired, swinging the M-63 from right to left. The slugs chopped the terrorists down, two of the five dying on their feet without having moved a single muscle, and the third falling with his hand on a pistol. The fourth hardman managed to draw his gun but crumpled under the leaden rain. Then the fifth, the man holding the tanto, darted behind Kuragin and held the sword to her throat.

The warrior let up on the trigger. All he could see of the Dragons terrorist was one foot and one ear.

For a few seconds no one moved. Kuragin simply stared, her relief obvious.

The hardman shifted so that one eye could study Bolan. "You are the one from last night. The one we were not able to kill."

Bolan offered no reply.

"You will drop your pistol or the woman dies," the terrorist said, pressing the blade lightly against Kuragin's neck to emphasize his demand. A thin red line formed on her skin.

"Kill her," Bolan said.

The terrorist was unable to hide his surprise. "You would stand there and let me slit her throat? You would let your own countryman die?"

"I'm not Russian," the warrior replied, stalling, waiting for the right moment, which was sure to come if he kept the man talking long enough. "I'm American."

"Whatever you are, I do not believe you want her harmed. You will put down your weapon and step back."

Kuragin spoke up. "Don't worry about me, Mike. Kill the son of a bitch and be done with it."

Hissing, the terrorist cuffed her on the back of the head. "Shut up, woman."

Bolan saw his chance. The Japanese had unwittingly exposed half of his face. But all at once, from the stairs outside, came the thud of fleet footsteps.

Reinforcements were on the way.

13

There were two of them. They had found the bodies near the elevator, and those of Ikano and the other man in the office, and rushed upstairs to warn their fellow Dragons. In their haste they burst through the door without thinking and were mowed down by the M-63.

The terrorist behind Kuragin had straightened and started to shout a warning as his companions appeared. The warning was strangled off by three more blasts of the machine pistol.

Bolan ran to the chair and used the tanto to cut the Russian free. "Can you walk?" he asked.

"I can try."

Her clothes were nowhere to be seen so Bolan stripped off his overcoat. "Here. Put this on. We have to get out of here before more show up."

Weak from her ordeal, Kuragin tried to comply. She slid her left arm into the coat but couldn't quite lift her right arm high enough. "Sprained it," she mumbled. "When they caught me."

The warrior helped, then looped an arm around her waist and braced her as she stood. She could barely stand, but she gritted her teeth and took uneven steps. He checked the stairs before descending. Kuragin had the presence of mind not to speak again until they were in the elevator.

"I want to thank you for saving me. I am in your debt. If there is ever anything I can do for you, you have but to ask."

"You could start telling me the truth for a change."

"I always have been honest with you."

"Not honest enough to let me know that you're Dorsakov's daughter." Bolan wedged the machine pistol under his jacket while watching the arrow on the floor indicator drop from the second to the first. "Keep your head down so no one can see how battered your face is," he directed. "Head straight for the entrance and don't stop for anyone or anything."

The door clanged open. Bolan ushered her past the secretary, who was on the phone. The woman glanced up, did a double take and turned.

"*Monsieur!* What is wrong with her? Where are you going? Did you see Mr. Ikano? He won't answer my calls."

"He's busy on the third floor. Give him an hour, then try again." Shoving on the glass doors, he hustled Kuragin to the car and held the passenger door open so she could slide in. Only when he was behind the wheel and driving from the parking lot did he allow himself to relax a little.

"I can't believe it was so easy," Kuragin stated.

"Neither can I." A second later he knew they had spoken too soon. A nondescript sedan had pulled out from beside the building and swung into position two cars behind them. "We have a tail," he announced.

"Can you lose them?"

"I can try." Bolan took a right at the next intersection. He stuck to the speed limit, acting as if he had no idea anyone was after them. The two Dragons made no attempt to overtake their car. He figured the terrorists were going to shadow them to their destination.

Bolan drew up at a red light at a broad avenue lined with traffic. He glanced at the side mirror. The Dragons were now three cars behind. When the light changed, he gunned the engine and roared into the avenue, forcing a jaywalker to scramble for safety. The speedometer surged. Somewhere a policeman's whistle shrilled, but he paid it no heed.

The Dragons pulled out of their lane, zipped past the cars in front of them and roared around the corner. The man on the passenger side rolled down his window and leaned out, a Steyr assault rifle tucked to his shoulder.

Bolan looked in the rearview mirror and saw a policeman rush into the avenue in front of the Dragons. The officer was blowing on his whistle and wildly waving his arms to get them to stop. The terrorist cut loose with the Steyr. Passersby screamed as the hapless policeman collapsed, oozing blood from a half-dozen wounds.

Another intersection loomed, and Bolan turned to the right. The streets were narrow, with lots of twists and turns. He thought it would be simple to lose the Dragons. But he didn't count on a stalled station wagon blocking the street.

The Executioner slammed on the brakes. The driver of the station wagon was trying to start it but all the motor did was growl and sputter. A quick glance over a shoulder showed Bolan that his pursuers had just turned the corner and would soon be on them. He cut the steering wheel sharply and floored the gas pedal, shooting between the station wagon and a picket fence.

The Dragons tried the same maneuver, but the driver misjudged the gap and their car crashed into the station wagon's fender. The furious Frenchman opened his door and hopped out. Shaking a fist and cursing them roundly, he stalked toward their vehicle but halted abruptly when the gunner pointed the rifle at him. The driver then backed up a few feet, shifted and swerved past the stalled station wagon.

By then Bolan was more than a block away and racking his brain for a way to give the terrorists the slip. He took a left at the next junction, a right at the one after that. Kuragin, he noticed, was as pale as a sheet and hanging on to the door for dear life. A look in the mirror revealed the Dragons were still after them.

An alley appeared. Bolan drove into it and immediately regretted doing so. It was a dead end. Braking, he jammed the car into reverse and stepped on the gas. As the car zipped back out into the street, the Steyr chattered. Rounds drilled into the rear quarter panel and spanged off the back bumper.

"What if they hit the gas tank?" Kuragin asked.

Bolan needed no reminder. He accelerated, swept past a car whose driver had stopped in alarm at the sound of the gunfire and zoomed down a straightaway.

The Dragons came on swiftly.

"Lend me your pistol and I will try to stop them," Kuragin said. "I am still weak but I can shoot."

"No," Bolan said. In her condition she would be lucky if she could hit the broad side of a barn. She might wind up wounding bystanders instead, and the warrior was determined not to embroil more innocent civilians in his personal war. He hung a right, took a curve too fast and had to fight the wheel to retain control.

The warrior looked into the mirror but saw no sign of the Dragons. He couldn't understand what had happened to them. Then he swept past another alley and the Dragons shot out of it, nearly hitting his car broadside. The Dragons streaked in behind him, riding his bumper.

"Get down!" Bolan said, a split second before the gunner shattered their rear window. He ducked low himself. Slugs punctured the windshield and ripped into the top of the seat. The warrior raised his head high enough to see above the dash, spotted another turn and took it. Slumped down as he was, he couldn't control the car as well as he would have liked. It slammed into a parked truck before he could straighten out.

The gunner had stopped firing, but only long enough to slap in a new magazine.

Bolan sped out of the side street into another avenue. He weaved furiously among the cars, trying to put as many as he could behind him so the gunner would be unable to get a clear shot. For a minute the strategy worked. Then a taxi abruptly pulled out in front of him. He had to brake or crash, and the Dragons used the ten-second delay to make up a lot of lost ground and opened fire.

All at once a shrieking siren rent the air. A police car was rapidly overtaking the terrorists, scattering traffic as drivers pulled aside to let it pass.

Bolan saw the terrorist with the Steyr twist. He gritted his teeth in frustration when the gunner peppered the police car's windshield. The policeman at the wheel slumped, and the car veered toward the sidewalk, out of control. Pedestrians bolted, but a few were too slow. The police car hurtled into them like a metal battering ram, grinding several under its wheels. It veered again, toward a store, and smashed into a window in a spectacular shower of glass and rubble.

More lives had been ruthlessly snuffed out, Bolan reflected grimly. He had to do something, or many others would suffer the same fate. Shifting, he pointed at the suitcase in the back seat. "There's an AKM in there. Get it out for me."

Kuragin nodded. Her movements were labored. She had to grab the handle with both hands, and nearly lost her grip as she pulled the suitcase up. Grunting with the effort, she succeeded in placing the suitcase on the seat between them, then unfastened the latches. She removed the Kalashnikov AKM and extended the folding stock.

Bolan took the assault rifle in his right hand. "Lie low," he advised, and when she obeyed, he swung the rifle around so that it pointed out the missing rear window. He rested it across the seat and waited.

Having disposed of the police, the Dragons came on swiftly. Engine thundering, they swept down on the warrior's vehicle and rammed it with their front bumper.

The jolt threw off Bolan's aim. The AKM was jerked to the left, but he compensated and stroked the trigger a fraction of an instant before the terrorist with the Steyr did the same. Rounds chewed into the seat and the roof. His own shots punched through the windshield of the other car and caught the gunner full in the chest. The hardman sagged. The Steyr clattered to the pavement and tumbled end over end. Immediately the driver steered to the left to get out of the line of fire. Bolan shifted the AKM and nailed him.

The other vehicle quickly lost momentum and came to a gradual stop in the middle of the avenue.

By then Bolan was turning onto another side street. He traveled a few blocks, pulled to the curb and turned off the ignition. "We have to ditch the car."

"Whatever you want." Kuragin sounded terribly weak.

The Executioner replaced the AKM in the suitcase and slid out. He walked around to her side and assisted her to stand. Crossing the street, he headed west, listening to the plaintive wail of multiple sirens as police closed in on the area from various directions.

The warrior looked about for somewhere to hide in case the police appeared. A taxi cruised past an intersection a block away, and he pumped his arm to get the driver's attention. For a moment he thought he had failed. Then the brake lights came on.

Hurrying Kuragin along, he settled her in the back seat and slid in beside her, the suitcase balanced on his lap. Bolan gave the driver the address of their hotel. The Frenchman glanced back at the Russian several times and finally asked in French if she was all right. *"Malade,"* Bolan said. "She's sick."

The driver drove faster.

The warrior had the driver stop a block from the hotel, climbed out and paid. He scanned both sides of the street intently but saw no lurkers in the shadows or occupied cars. The lobby was practically empty, the desk clerk reading a magazine.

Kuragin held out until the door to their room closed behind them. Then, uttering a low groan, she collapsed and would have fallen had Bolan not caught her. He placed her on the bed and felt her forehead for a fever, often an early sign of internal damage. She had none.

After depositing the suitcase in the closet, Bolan went out, locked the door and hastened to the phone on the front desk. It gave him pause when he was told that Brognola wasn't in. "When do you expect him back?"

"He left no instructions in that regard," the woman at the other end answered. "Would you care to leave a message?"

"No, thanks. I'll try again later." Bolan was disappointed. He would have liked to compare notes and learn the latest developments.

An old candy machine sat in one corner. Bolan bought several chocolate bars and took them upstairs. Kuragin was in the deep sleep of total exhaustion. He folded the ragged bedspread over her to keep her warm and sank into the only chair.

Someone knocked lightly on the door.

The Executioner was there in a moment, the Desert Eagle out and cocked. "Who is it?" he asked softly.

"Pizza delivery," Hal Brognola's deep voice rumbled.

The big Fed grinned when Bolan admitted him, but the grin faded promptly when he saw the Russian agent. "Is she all right?"

"The Red Dragons roughed her up pretty bad. She's tough, though. She'll pull through." Bolan locked the door and leaned against the wall. "I just tried to reach you on the phone. You must have important news if you came here in person."

Brognola moved to the bed. He listened to the woman breathe, assuring himself she was indeed sound asleep. Still not satisfied, he motioned at the dirty window at the other end of the room and walked over behind the warrior. "A lot has happened," he admitted quietly. "I figured I'd best come in person."

Bolan peered out the window and saw a black sedan near the front entrance. "Yours?"

Brognola nodded. "I brought four of my men along in case there's a need for firepower. With all the terrorists and Russian operatives roaming the streets looking for Dorsakov, it's not safe for someone in our line of work to be out and about."

"Tell me about it," Bolan stated dryly.

"To cases," Brognola said. "First, the big news. We now know for a fact that Dorsakov is still in Paris. He was spotted, with Roskov, at the Bastille subway station early this morning by one of the Russian teams scouring Paris. Shots were exchanged, and two of the agents took some lead. Dorsakov and Roskov escaped."

"Any clues as to where we can find them?"

"Not yet. I have every person I can spare working on this, so it's only a matter of time. But we're racing against the clock." Brognola turned somber. "The Russians have brought in a lot of their people, too. A conservative estimate would be close to fifty. I suspect they've pulled in every agent they can spare from all over Europe. They're tearing Paris upside down and leaving no stone unturned."

"Will you inform them that we've recovered Marya?"

"Not just yet," the big Fed replied. "I'd like you to have a chance to talk to her first. See if you can find out a little more about her relationship with her father, or anything else that might help us."

"That's a job for your people."

"If we took her in and questioned her, the Russians would complain, through channels, and I'd be called on the carpet." Brognola shook his head. "I'd rather keep it informal. If you don't learn anything, we're no worse off than we are right this minute."

"I'll do what I can."

Brognola straightened. "For the duration I'm working out of the embassy. If you need me, call me there." He glanced around the shabby room. "And if I were you, I'd get out of this dump as soon as she comes around. The Russians know you're here, and they might get it into their heads to pay you an unexpected visit."

"Point taken."

"By the way, where's that car I had delivered? I didn't see it out front."

Briefly Bolan told about his run-in with the Red Dragons.

"Sorry to hear about the policemen and those civilians," Brognola said. "But that's what happens when fanatics like the Silver Crescent and the Dragons are on the loose." He headed for the door. "I'll get in touch with the Japanese. Ikano maintained offices and another residence in Tokyo. They'll want to go through both from top to bottom. My guess is that thanks to you they'll be able to put an end to the Red Dragons once and for all."

Bolan followed and nodded at the Russian. "As soon as she's up and around, we'll be moving to another hotel. She might have told her superiors that I'm staying here, and I don't want them taking another crack at me."

Brognola paused with the door open and gazed at Kuragin. "Why do I have the feeling that she's the key to settling this mess?" He stepped into the hall and looked both ways. "Stay frosty, my friend."

"Always."

Bolan locked the door, turned off the light and sat in the chair, facing the bed. Until Mikhail Dorsakov's hiding place was found, he had little to do except cool his heels. Resting his chin on his forearms, he allowed himself to doze.

A whisper of noise brought the warrior around. He opened his eyes to find Kuragin staring at him. Outside, evening had fallen, and the room was shrouded in gloom. "How do you feel?" he asked.

"I ache all over. But I will live." She sat up stiffly, then stretched. "You should not have let me sleep so long."

"You needed the rest," Bolan pointed out.

Kuragin looked down at herself. She still wore his overcoat, buttoned almost to her neck. "I wish I had a spare change of clothes."

"We'll go buy you some," Bolan offered, "after you answer a few questions."

"I would rather they wait."

"They can't," the warrior stated, sitting up. "For starters, you can explain why Russian Intelligence had a hit squad waiting to nail us the moment we set down at Orly."

"So you found out. I told my superiors it was unwise to try and take you out. But they would not listen to me." She slid to the edge of the bed and sat, staring glumly at the floor. "They tried to kill you because they want to dispose of the traitor themselves. The renegade is Russian, after all. They regard this affair as an internal matter, and they resent any outside interference."

"It won't wash," Bolan said. "Your own president ordered your agency to cooperate with us. There has to be more. What aren't you telling me?"

Kuragin glanced up. She gnawed on her lower lip a moment, then said, "I cannot see what harm it would do to admit the truth. And I do owe you my life." She took a deep breath. "My superiors are very worried that you might take the traitor alive."

"What does it matter so long as we get our hands on the Novichok-5?"

"He knows things. Lots of very important secrets that the agency would not like to become common knowledge."

Now it made sense, Bolan realized. The Russians wanted him out of the way so they could nab Dorsakov themselves and make certain the man never talked. "Why did you kill those two agents in the alley behind the café?"

"Two reasons. One, because I was afraid you would not kill them outright yourself but might leave one breathing so you could question him and learn the truth. And two, because they nearly shot me, if you'll recall. I was not sure if they were only after you, or after both of us."

"Why would the agency want you dead?"

"Who can say? You know how deceitful people in the spy business can be. The left hand often does not know what the right is doing. There might be those who want me out of the way because of who I am."

"Which brings me to the big question," Bolan said. "Why didn't you admit that you're Dorsakov's daughter?"

"Again, I was under orders. My superiors did not want your side exploiting it to lure—" she stopped speaking and seemed to wrestle with herself "—my father into a trap."

Bolan was skeptical. It could just as easily be that the Russians were more afraid of having the Novichok-5 fall into American hands than Dorsakov himself. But he let her claim go unchallenged for the time being. "All right. Let's say I buy all you've told me. It doesn't explain one last thing." He locked eyes with her. "Why you? Why did the agency send Dorsakov's own daughter after him?"

"Because I volunteered."

"Again, why?"

"Wouldn't you, if your father had betrayed your country and everything you stood for? He not only branded himself for the shameless traitor he is, but he put me under suspicion, as well, simply by virtue of the fact that I am his daughter." Kuragin's strained voice lowered to a whisper. "Within two hours of the theft, the agency had put me under arrest. They felt I must have had a part in planning and carrying out my father's plan. Four days and nights they questioned me. They used polygraphs. They drugged me. And finally they took me at my word even though some still had their doubts."

Bolan knew enough about Russian interrogation techniques to appreciate the living hell she had gone through.

"I was told I would be set free, but that I could no longer work for the agency. My record had been tarnished by my father's actions." She closed her eyes. "They made it plain that there was only one way I could prove myself to them."

The warrior saw where her story was leading. "So they made you a deal?"

Kuragin nodded. "They would be willing to reinstate me and all would be forgiven if I would hunt down my father and mete out the justice he deserves."

It was despicable, Bolan mused. Didn't she realize they were simply using her to silence a potential leak and recover their precious biochemical weapon? Her superiors didn't care about her personal feelings. He could see that it was tearing her up inside, and he wanted to press the point, to get her to see that she was a puppet on a string. But suddenly, in the hallway, the sole of a foot lightly scraped the floor and there was a faint click, as of a gun safety being released.

His enemies had found him.

14

The Executioner ran to the closet and hauled out the suitcase. He saw the doorknob move a fraction as whoever had crept down the hall tested to see if the door was locked.

Kuragin had risen, her eyes wide. She backed over to him and whispered, "I can help. Give me a gun."

Bolan had the AKM in his hands. He ejected the magazine and inserted another, then reached for the M-63 machine pistol to give it to her. But there was no time. At a bellowed command in the corridor, the door caved in under a tremendous blow, the hinges ripping from the jamb as it fell inward with a resounding crash.

A pair of brawny gunners had used their shoulders to gain entry. Side by side they stumbled into the room, halted and extended pistols. And side by side they were mowed down by a burst from the Kalashnikov. Another triggerman appeared in the doorway, an AK-47 tucked to his side. He got off a short burst that stitched the wall above the warrior's head even as Bolan's own burst turned him into a sieve.

The warrior ran to the doorway, crouched and peered outside. The hall was temporarily empty except for the body.

Kuragin claimed the M-63, moved to one of the fallen gunners and picked up his pistol. "A Makarov," she said bitterly. "These men are Russian agents."

"They were," Bolan amended, standing. "Stick close. We're going out the back way." He eased out, hearing a commotion in the lobby. It sounded as if the desk clerk were yelling. A door slammed and a woman cursed.

The Executioner retreated toward the back stairs, covering Kuragin as she emerged on his heels. Thanks to a burned-out light bulb, the stairs were plunged in shadow. Bolan hesitated, scouring the darkness, leery of walking into a trap.

"Someone is coming up from the lobby," Kuragin whispered.

Further delay could prove costly. Bolan descended, his back scraping the wall. At the bottom was a door that opened onto a small lot littered with garbage cans and discarded household items. He sped across the lot to an alley and turned to the right.

Kuragin suddenly gave a low cry and nearly stumbled. She lifted her left leg to examine her foot, saying, "I'm sorry. I think I stepped on glass."

Bolan had forgotten she had no shoes. He hurried her along to the street. Since they couldn't very well go strolling along a busy sidewalk with the assault rifle, he removed the magazine and stashed it in a garbage can. Kuragin hid the smaller M-63 under her coat. Then they headed due east. Ahead a taxi appeared, parked by a fruit stand. Bolan ushered her into the back seat while the driver was busy buying apples. When the man climbed back in, Bolan told her, "Have him take us somewhere you can buy clothes."

The Frenchman was the gabby sort and kept up a running conversation with the woman about the delights of the city. The store he picked was on a quiet street lined with other small establishments.

Bolan sat in a chair while Marya bought jeans, a blouse and sandals. When she came out of the changing room, she had the machine pistol wrapped up in the overcoat, which she handed over to him. After they paid and were walking from the store, she hooked her arm in his.

"So what now?"

"We find a new hotel and I get word to Brognola," Bolan answered. "Then there's nothing else we can do but wait for your father to slip up and hope we reach him before your agency friends or any of the terrorists do."

"Were it not for the fact we must retrieve the Novichok-5 at all costs, I would not care who found him first just so he is eliminated."

"Do you really mean that about your own father?"

"Of course. What difference does that make? I have a job to do, as do you. Personal allegiances do not enter into the picture."

Bolan saw the hint of pain deep in her eyes. "I think you're lying. I think you do care for him."

"You are mistaken," she replied icily. "I would care if he had been like most fathers and spent time raising me, but he was never home, never there when I wanted or needed him. His work kept him so busy that my mother often said that she had a ghost for a husband. Well, the same applies to me. I had a ghost for a father. I have no feelings for him at all."

"You never did anything together?" Bolan asked idly while surveying the street for the opposition.

"Oh, every now and then we would go for a walk in the park. Several times we went on vacations. Once we even came to Paris."

Bolan glanced at her. "When?"

"I was eight or nine at the time."

"What did you do while you were here?"

"The usual tourist things. We visited the Eiffel Tower and other landmarks, strolled along the Seine, saw the Louvre. I remember walking across one of the bridges, and feeding the pigeons in a park. It was one of the few times we were ever a normal family."

"What else did you do?" Bolan pressed her.

Kuragin, lost in her memories, didn't notice his urgency. "We went to a department store. Father bought Mother some perfume." She stopped, gazing dreamily into the past. "And we visited the islands, too. Oh, and the Catacombs. Father was particularly interested in them, although Mother and I didn't care for all those old bones. It was upsetting for a child my age."

Bolan halted in midstride. The Catacombs were a huge network of tunnels under the city, so vast that they had never been fully explored. At one time the tunnels had served as burial grounds for overflow from the cemeteries. It was estimated more than six million people had been laid to rest down there. Part of the Catacombs were now a tourist attraction for those whose tastes ran to the macabre.

"What's the matter? Why did you stop?"

"We need another taxi," Bolan said, and hurried to the next wide avenue. They didn't have long to wait before one came by. When the driver asked for their destination, the warrior responded simply, "The Catacombs."

Kuragin swung toward him. "Surely you are not thinking what I think you are thinking?"

"Why not? Your father isn't about to stay at a hotel. He knows that every one will be alerted to keep watch for someone answering his description. And we know he's not using old safehouses."

"But the Catacombs? No one lives down there."

"He doesn't have to stay there forever, just until everyone has given up hunting for him." Bolan placed the folded overcoat in his lap. "I admit it's a long shot, but it's the only one we have. It won't hurt for us to take a look."

At 2 Place Denfert-Rochereau the taxi let them off. The next tour was in half an hour, and Bolan signed them up. They stood under a sign that read Stop, This Is The Empire Of Death, until the time came to go down. Eighteen tourists from various countries were in the group so it was easy for Bolan to drift to the back where he could study the branching corridors as they went along.

Kuragin, for all her courage, was ill at ease.

In a way, Bolan couldn't blame her. He'd seen more than his share of death and dead bodies, but never anything to compare to the sight of hundreds upon hundreds of ancient bones and leering skulls lining the dusty walls for mile after mile.

Bolan was counting on a long shot and knew it. Only a small portion of the Catacombs was open to the general public. The rest were clearly marked off-limits. He hoped to find a branch tunnel not in regular use but which bore recent footprints, but he soon found his idea impractical.

The tour guide droned on and on about the long history of the Catacombs. Bolan discovered that some of the branching tunnels were blocked off, while others weren't. Quite a few bore footprints in the dust. So many, in fact, that to check every one would take weeks.

"If my father is down here, we will never find him," Kuragin said, seeming to read the warrior's mind.

By this time they had fallen a dozen feet behind the tour group. Bolan went to catch up, then slowed on seeing a figure break away from a side tunnel and merge in with the rest. The man moved so swiftly and surely that no one noticed. In the dim light Bolan couldn't make out the man's features, not at first. A minute passed and the glow from a light caught the man in profile.

"Roskov!" Kuragin hissed, taking a stride forward.

"No." Bolan gripped her wrist to stop her from doing something rash. "Not yet." The tour group went around a turn. The warrior halted and pulled her into the shadows. "We'll wait here for him to return."

"Do you think he will?"

"I know it," Bolan said, and sought a sheltered nook where they could hide. Kuragin hesitated when it came to stepping over a skeleton into the dark cranny he picked.

"I know I'm being childish, but this place bothers me greatly."

The Executioner gazed along the tunnel at the long line of bones and wondered if that was how Paris would look if the Novichok-5 were used. He was impressed by Dorsakov's clever choice of a place to hide. No one would have thought to search for the rogue in the bowels of the city. It was sheer luck, their being at the right place in the right time to spot Roskov.

The voice of the tour guide gradually receded in the distance. A deathly stillness gripped the tunnels. The bones gleamed dully in the pale light. Bolan unwrapped the AKM and checked the magazine by feel. Half of the thirty rounds it held were left.

For a long time neither of them spoke. It was Kuragin who broke the silence by whispering, "I have a request to make of you, Mike Belasko."

"Which is?"

"I want the honor of killing my father. Roskov is yours, but you must promise me that you will let me dispose of the traitor."

"No can do."

"Why not?"

"There are too many lives at stake for me to let you turn this into a personal vendetta. Getting the case with the vials is all that really counts. Killing your father comes second, and it doesn't matter who does it."

"I beg to differ. Were it not for him, none of the lives you mention would be at risk. I am under orders to dispose of him, and dispose of him I shall."

Bolan looked at her. In the murky confines of their nook her face was no more than a vague pale patch. "If you get a clear shot, fine. Just don't let your feelings cloud your judgment. We can't risk him getting away."

"He won't. I guarantee you."

Neither broke the quiet again. Their wait dragged on and on. Bolan began to wonder if he had erred and Roskov would never show. Then a droning voice sounded in the distance, a different tour guide leading yet another bunch of tourists. He listened to the patter of their footsteps and ducked low when shadows danced on the tunnel walls.

The tour group slowly filed past. It was larger than before, more than twenty all told, and prominent among them was Roskov. He carried a brown grocery bag and wore a cap pulled low over his brow.

Bolan let the group go by, then crept forward on his hands and knees. When the gawking tourists were fifty feet away, Roskov drifted toward the rear, pretending to study the skeletons on either side. Seventy feet, and Roskov darted into a side tunnel so swiftly that no one noticed.

The warrior wondered how many times Roskov and Dorsakov had done the same over the past few days. It was strange the tour guides hadn't caught on since they made the trek a dozen times daily. Maybe, he reflected, Dorsakov had paid one or two of them to insure their silence.

Bolan drew back into the nook and waited for the group to make its return trip. Kuragin might have been sculpted from marble for all the life she showed. He had no idea what was going through her mind, but he did know he had to watch her like a hawk once they left their hiding place.

At length the guide led his awed flock back toward the entrance. The warrior emerged, worked the bolt of the AKM and moved toward the branch Roskov had taken. It was dark, like the inside of a cave, but not so dark he couldn't see once his eyes adjusted. Bolan went in warily, alert for booby traps. He set each foot down lightly, but in the total silence of the Catacombs even light footfalls made noise.

Behind him came Marya Kuragin, her face the color of chalk, her grip on the machine pistol so tight her knuckles were also white. She was strung as tight as barbed wire, and it wouldn't take much for her to snap.

Bolan saw a bend ahead. He listened but heard no voices. A glance showed a long, straight stretch that seemed to recede into a void. Finding the Russians wasn't going to be simple. He paused many times to test the air with his ears and his nose. In time he was rewarded with the faint but definite scent of tobacco.

A junction appeared. There were three branches to choose from, and Bolan went from one to the other, inhaling deeply. The scent was strongest in the middle branch. He walked into it, more cautiously than ever, aware he was stalking into the lair of two old pros who weren't likely to miss a trick.

Even keyed as the warrior was for the unexpected, he nearly missed seeing the trip wire. Had he not stopped to glance at his companion, then down at his feet when he went on, he would have been blown to kingdom come. A black wire stood out against the background of lighter stones underneath. He froze with his right foot partially raised.

Kuragin was staring straight ahead and started to go past him.

Like lightning, Bolan's hand flicked out and stopped her. He pointed at the wire, then lifted his foot over it. Once she had followed his example, he traced the wire to the side wall and found it attached to a POMZ-2M antipersonnel mine that had been partially imbedded in the wall. It was a small mine, much like a hand grenade in size and shape, but it packed enough explosive to maim or kill in a sixty-foot radius.

Motioning at Kuragin, Bolan resumed the lead. Fifty feet farther he came on a second trip wire, again attached to an antipersonnel mine.

Remembering the elaborate security system at the château, the warrior could only hope there were no motion or heat sensors along the tunnel. He advanced for a short span, then stopped at the sight of a glimmer of light on the left side of the tunnel.

Suddenly Kuragin shot past him.

Bolan snatched at her shoulder, but she wrenched loose and quickened her pace, her obsession blinding her to the grave mistake she was making. She broke into a run. The Executioner did the same, overtaking her swiftly. Hoping against hope that Dorsakov and Roskov wouldn't hear, he slung the AKM, flung himself forward and tackled her.

The woman went down, but only to her knees. Twisting, she drove the stock of the machine pistol at the warrior's head. Bolan dodged, then scrambled aside as she tried to kick him. He knew he had to end their clash swiftly or they would lose the element of surprise. Lunging, he seized hold of the M-63 and tried to tear it from her grasp. Kuragin almost caught him off guard by butting her forehead at his chin. He pulled back in time, pivoted and did the only thing he could do—he punched her on the jaw.

She crumpled soundlessly. Bolan caught her and eased her down. He was straightening when a hard object was jammed into his nape and a flinty voice addressed him.

"Do not move, American, or you die."

Bolan froze. It wasn't Dorsakov, and he well knew that Roskov would have no compunctions about putting a bullet in his brain if he so much as quivered. The man was a pro in every sense of the word. Twice now Roskov had taken him by surprise, a feat few men could do even once. He felt a rough hand frisk him, heard his hardware being set aside. Then the pressure on his neck eased.

"You will pick her up, stand and turn."

Again, Bolan complied. Roskov held the Walther P-5, his expression as stony as the walls.

"Walk straight ahead."

The light came from a lantern hung on a wall in a circular chamber lined with niches filled with bones. A pair of sleeping bags were spread out beside the wall. Near them were two backpacks. In the middle of the chamber sat a small folding table and two folding chairs. Mikhail Dorsakov was playing solitaire and looked up as the warrior entered.

"So Sergei was right," the renegade said blandly. His gaze moved to Kuragin, and he shot up out of the chair as if fired from a catapult. "No! What has happened to her, American?" he demanded as he rushed over.

The Executioner saw no need to hold back the truth. "Your daughter was rushing in here to kill you. I had to stop her."

Dorsakov touched his daughter's brow, then gestured sharply at the sleeping bags. "Set her down, please." He went to the backpack and took out a thermos which he brought over as his daughter was being lowered to the ground. "How badly did you hurt her?"

"I had to tap her on the chin. I didn't want to, but she wasn't about to listen to reason. Her superiors have told her that the only way she can clear her name is if she kills you."

"The bastards," Dorsakov said, flushing with anger. His eyes narrowed. "What is your name, American?"

"Belasko."

"And how is it, Mr. Belasko, that you know she is my daughter, and about her being a spy?"

"We've been working together since you escaped from the château," Bolan explained. "Those bruises on her face were put there by the Red Dragons. They got their hands on her and were trying to persuade her to tell them where they would find you when I stepped in.''

"Then I am in your debt twice," Dorsakov said, and indicated a chair. "Take a seat." Kneeling, he started to unscrew the thermos cap, but hesitated, his lips pursed. "Perhaps it would be best if I waited to revive her. Knowing how strong-willed she can be, she might try to eliminate me before I have a chance to explain myself.''

Bolan sat and propped his hands on his knees. His mind raced as he tried to think of a way out of the fix Kuragin had placed him in. He saw that Roskov had moved to one side and had the Walther fixed on his forehead.

"I need answers, Mr. Belasko," Dorsakov said. "Why is it that the two of you were sent after me when I specifically warned about the dire consequences that would occur if I were not left alone?''

"Did you really think they would leave you be, given what's at stake?''

Dorsakov pondered a bit. "No, I suppose not. It was naive of me. But it was also naive of them to think I would not carry out my threat.''

"Meaning?''

The rogue didn't answer. Instead, Dorsakov rested a hand on his daughter's shoulder. "My sweet little Marya. I never thought the agency would hold you to blame. I am sorry for what they must have put you through.''

"Why not make it easy on her, and on yourself?'' Bolan said. "Give up now while you still can. Hand over the Novichok-5 before it's too late.''

"Mr. Belasko, please. I may be naive now and then, but I'm not stupid." Dorsakov snorted. "To whom should I turn myself over to? Russian Intelligence? We both know that RI plays the same games as its predecessor. Or perhaps you would rather I surrender to you and be taken into American custody. In which case I will be branded a traitor by my countrymen, and poor Marya will be made to suffer.''

''You're already branded a traitor,'' the warrior pointed out. ''And you could bring Marya with you. Ask for asylum. It's the only way both of you will get out of this alive.'' As he talked, Bolan scanned the chamber for the case containing the Novichok-5. At first he failed to spot it. Then a stray glimmer of light drew his gaze to the nearest niche. The case lay amid a heap of old bones.

''What makes you think I care all that much about living?'' Dorsakov responded softly. ''If I cannot have my revenge, nothing else matters.''

''Not even your daughter?''

Dorsakov looked up. ''Do not try to twist my thoughts, Mr. Belasko. Of course I care for her. But I have gone too far now to turn back. And Marya would never agree to asking for asylum. She is, if anything, more patriotic than I ever was. Mother Russia is her first love and always will be.''

Bolan tried to come up with an argument the rogue would accept. But before he could, he saw Roskov stiffen and cock his head.

''Mikhail.''

''*Da?*''

''Men come. Many men, with guns.''

15

The Executioner could do nothing except sit there helplessly as the rustle of stealthy movement filled the tunnel. All his weapons had been left outside the chamber. He glanced around for others that might be handy, but there was none.

Roskov scowled. "This one brought them!" he declared, aiming the Walther at Bolan. "Let me kill him now, Mikhail, and be done with it!"

For a few anxious seconds the warrior thought his time had come. He would try to leap aside, but there wasn't a man alive whose reflexes were faster than a speeding bullet.

"No," Dorsakov said, rushing to the entrance. "We might be able to use him as a hostage."

The rustling ceased. Someone approached quite close to the opening, making no attempt to hide the fact, and then stopped. A hard-as-nails voice called out in thickly accented English. "Mikhail Dorsakov, I know you are in there! You will submit, now, or suffer the consequences."

Bolan watched Dorsakov and Roskov exchange furious looks. The latter faced the tunnel.

"Is that you, Varna?"

"It is I, Mikhail. I would like to talk to you. Unarmed, naturally."

Roskov leaned toward Dorsakov and whispered in Russian. Dorsakov absently answered, "I do not trust him, either. But we must hear what he has to say."

For the moment they had completely forgotten about Bolan. The warrior glanced at Kuragin, who still lay unconscious, then at the metal case. He was so close, yet the Novichok-5 might as well be on the moon for all the good it did him.

The man in the tunnel called out again. "What will it be, Mikhail? Will you hear me out, or do we just come in there and get you?"

Dorsakov drew a Makarov from under his jacket and backed up until he was next to the table. "You may come in, Varna, but keep your hands where we can see them. Sergei would like nothing better than to end your vile career here and now."

Bolan had to shift to see the tall, muscular man in a suit and tie who strolled into the chamber with an air of cold arrogance. The newcomer gave Roskov a look of sheer contempt and turned toward Dorsakov.

"So we meet again," Varna said.

"Have you forgotten our mother tongue?" Dorsakov asked. "In the past you only liked to use English when you had no other choice, as I recall."

"Or when it is expedient." Varna wagged his head at the walls. "These tunnels might be infested by winos and other such rabble. Who knows when prying ears might overhear, eh? If all they hear is English, they can hardly identify us, now can they?"

"I see. Perhaps I should shout out that you are a Russian agent for the benefit of anyone who might be in earshot."

"Feel free," Varna said, unruffled, "but we have more important matters to discuss." His hawkish eyes swept to the case as if drawn by a magnet. "You know what we have come for. Hand it over and we will permit you to leave unmolested."

Dorsakov leaned against the table. "We will get to that in a moment. First I would like to know how you found us."

"What difference does it make?"

"Humor me."

Varna folded his arms. "Your daughter led us here. But don't hold it against her. She had no idea she was doing so."

"You followed her?"

"And run the risk of being spotted? Credit us with more intelligence than that. No, we were homed in on the frequency of the transmitter planted on her. It has a range of two miles, so we were able to stay a discreet distance behind. She never knew."

Bolan spoke up. "He's lying, Dorsakov. I happen to know your daughter bought a whole new change of clothes before we came to the Catacombs. They haven't had a chance to plant a thing on her."

Varna smiled. "Who said we planted it on her *clothes*, American?" he taunted. "The bug was implanted during an interrogation she underwent back in Russia. It was inserted while she was unconscious, and she has no idea it is there."

"Implanted?" Dorsakov repeated, looking at Marya. The full meaning seemed to hit him with the force of a physical blow. "You pig!" he snapped. "My own daughter!"

"It was not my idea. Nor was I the one who performed the insertion," Varna stated calmly. "And since when have you objected to standard procedure? You know how it works, Mikhail. We needed to keep track of her, and this was the best way. Unfortunately we lost her when the Dragons abducted her, and were unable to locate her again until she returned to the hotel where she stayed with your American friend.''

Now Bolan knew how the Russian hit squad had been able to latch on to them so quickly at Orly and find them again no matter how hard he tried to ditch the gunners. And all the time he had thought the bug was in the car!

''Well, now that you have found us, what next?'' Dorsakov asked. ''I know you are not going to let us walk out if I give you the Novichok-5, no matter what you claim.''

''All we want are the vials,'' Varna stated. ''We have no interest in you.''

''Regrettably you will not get either,'' Dorsakov replied, moving around the table to the niche containing the case. He picked it up, squatted and laid it flat on the ground.

''What are you doing?'' Varna asked.

Dorsakov slipped the pistol into its holster, opened the special container and removed one of the vials. Holding it as he might a delicate egg, he closed the case, then stood, the case in his other hand.

The warrior had been tensed to leap, to stop the container from being opened, but Roskov was too alert.

''You're insane,'' Varna said.

Bolan had a different opinion. Dorsakov was taking a desperate gamble that might well result in all their deaths and the deaths of hundreds of thousands aboveground if the Novichok-5 seeped out into the streets.

''Call it what you will,'' Dorsakov said. ''But unless you want to die, you will call off your men and leave.

And you will not dare show yourselves again or, so help me, I will drop the vial."

Varna frowned. "I can't do that, Mikhail."

"Why not? Do you want to perish?"

"Of course not. But I have my orders. And if I let you escape, I might as well pack my bags for Siberia."

Someone in the tunnel called out in Russian. Varna's men were becoming impatient. At the shout, Roskov stared out the entrance, and Bolan rose, taking a stride toward Dorsakov. Only Dorsakov spied him and whirled, raising the vial aloft.

"Not another step, Mr. Belasko. I am not bluffing."

Bolan halted, his hands out from his sides.

Dorsakov moved slowly toward the opening. "The moment of truth is upon us, Varna. Either move out of the way or prepare to die. I no longer care one way or the other what happens to me."

"What about your daughter?" Varna asked, worry in his tone at last. "Don't you care what happens to her?"

To everyone's surprise, it was Kuragin herself who answered. "Yes, Father dearest. What about me?"

Bolan looked, and realized the situation had gone from bad to worse. She was rising, the pistol she had taken from the dead agent at the hotel in her right hand, aimed at her father. Everyone else froze. Even Roskov, for once, appeared uncertain whether he should shoot to save Dorsakov.

Varna moved first, taking a step toward her. "Stay out of this, woman! You have already caused us enough trouble by helping the American get away from us. And do not try to deny it. Witnesses saw you shoot our men at that café."

"Shut up," Kuragin ordered, and shot him.

The slug slammed into Varna's chest, knocking him backward. He staggered into the tunnel, clutched in vain at the wall for support, tried to speak and fell.

"You should not have done that, daughter," Dorsakov said.

"Who are you to tell me what to do?" Kuragin barked, her once lovely features contorted in rabid hatred. "Thanks to you, I was arrested, beaten and tortured. Thanks to you, I was humiliated beyond endurance. You are nothing but a traitor, and you deserve to die!"

Bolan knew she was close to breaking. Her last words had been shrieked at the top of her lungs. Once she fired, he had to catch the vial before it hit the earth. There was only one problem. Dorsakov was eight feet away. It would be close. Too close.

The next instant a projectile streaked into the chamber, struck the ceiling with a resounding thud and clattered to the floor, spewing tear gas. It was the signal for all hell to break loose.

At a harsh shout in the tunnel, two men charged into the chamber, subguns up and ready. They saw Dorsakov holding the vial and drew up short in stark panic. Neither noticed Roskov, over by the wall. His Walther spoke twice, dropping both. Then he swung toward Bolan.

But the warrior was already in motion. Whirling, he ran toward a niche and leapt, landing hard on the jumbled bones as the Walther cracked twice more. The bullets smacked into the lip of the niche, missing him by a handbreadth.

Roskov started toward him but halted as the cloud of tear gas billowed upward, filling the middle of the chamber and spreading swiftly.

"We must get out of here!" Dorsakov yelled, making for the entrance.

"No!" Kuragin yelled. She extended her pistol, but the next instant was engulfed by the tear gas.

The Executioner could see none of them. He heard a muffled shout, a shot, the sound of a blow landing, then a scraping noise, as of a heavy body being dragged. Taking a deep breath before the tear gas reached him, he pushed up out of the niche and dropped to the floor. In the tunnel more shouts were punctuated by gunfire, both subguns and pistols blasting away. Staying low to the ground and squinting to keep the gas from stinging his eyes, he scuttled past the chairs and the table. Most of the cloud was above him but settling rapidly. Dimly he saw the entrance ahead.

Suddenly a pair of shoes materialized, the toes pointing into the chamber. Bolan stopped. A man coughed lightly and turned to escape the gas. The Executioner pushed himself up, his outstretched hands catching hold of a jacket. His shoulder rammed into the small of the man's back and they hurtled into the far wall of the tunnel, falling on top of Varna.

His adversary was a Russian agent. Bolan swept into a crouch, pivoted and drove the flat of his palm into the man's nose as the Russian tried to bring up an Uzi. Cartilage crunched. The man sagged, dazed.

The Executioner tore the Uzi loose, reversed his grip and drilled a half-dozen rounds into the agent's chest.

Intuition screamed at Bolan to move and he did, throwing himself onto his back as another subgun chattered. Rounds sliced the air above him. Twisting, he saw another Russian, this one holding a MAC-10. The warrior stroked the Uzi's trigger, and a burst of 9 mm rounds punched the man onto his face.

Bolan looked both ways, seeking Dorsakov and his daughter. Three other bodies lay in the tunnel, all Russian agents. A dozen yards past the chamber was another junction. Since that was the only way that Dorsakov could have gone, the Executioner rose to give chase but paused when he saw the electronic instrument slung over the shoulder of one of the dead men.

Mentally crossing his fingers that it wasn't damaged, Bolan darted to the body and slid the leather sling free. The instrument was the size of a small transistor radio but with a small circular screen at the top, a proximity indicator underneath and four large buttons below. It had been manufactured in Russia.

Bolan rose and headed in pursuit. He would rather not have to rely on the tracer since he rarely had cause to use one, but it might well be his sole link to Dorsakov and the Novichok-5.

At the junction it was easy to spot the route they had taken. Fresh footprints in the dust showed that he should bear to the right.

It soon became apparent that Dorsakov was looping around to the main tunnel used by the tours. Bolan thought to check the Uzi while on the fly and learned the magazine had four rounds left. Four rounds, and he had both Dorsakov and Roskov to deal with. Not to mention Kuragin.

Forty minutes went by before the main tunnel came into sight. Bolan headed for street level, pacing himself. Figures moved in the distance, or he thought they did. Soon the exit appeared, so he hid the Uzi under his jacket. But he need not have worried. The tours were over for the day; the building was deserted. One of the front doors had been kicked open.

The night air felt cool on the warrior's brow. He scoured the street and the parking area but saw no one. Nor were there any taxis in the vicinity.

Bolan jogged toward the closest avenue, aware that every moment he delayed was a moment Dorsakov got farther away. He assumed Kuragin would be in pursuit of her father, and if the Russians traveled beyond the range of the tracer, the odds of the Executioner finding Dorsakov again were next to nil.

At the corner Bolan halted and looked for a taxi. He saw one, but it carried a passenger and went on by. Stepping out into the flow of traffic, he blocked the path of the next cab, which had its overhead light off. The driver was too surprised to do more than sputter as Bolan ran to the back door and slid in.

"Excusez-moi—" the flustered cabdriver began.

Bolan pulled out the Uzi but made a point of not aiming at the driver. He had no need to. The man immediately drove on, rattling off a stream of abuse in French.

"Be quiet a moment," Bolan growled, nestling the tracer in his lap. He fiddled with the four buttons, turning one after the other until the screen lighted up, displaying a grid. The proximity indicator didn't register at all. He tried each knob again and suddenly the red needle rose, but not much. Fine tuning moved it a hair more.

Bolan stared at the grid. A tiny green blip was near the top, to the left, almost off the screen. "That way," he urged, pointing in the direction they had to go.

The driver was too intrigued to protest. He turned left at the next intersection.

The blip moved a bit nearer the center of the grid. Bolan nodded and continued to direct the driver as needed. The red needle showed he was indeed gaining ground but very slowly.

One of Paris's many bridges appeared in the distance, decked with lights. It meant they were nearing the Seine River. Bolan was relieved to note that the blip stayed stationary, indicating Dorsakov had stopped.

The taxi turned onto a side street that paralleled the shimmering Seine, and the proximity needle pegged. The warrior told the driver to stop. A glance at the meter told him how much the fare should be, but he paid the driver twice as much on the off chance it would induce the man not to run to the police.

The Uzi under his jacket, Bolan got out. The moment the door closed, the taxi sped off. To the warrior's right stood a row of quaint homes. To his left, the gurgling river. He moved cautiously, studying the houses, convinced those he sought were in one of them. The blip in the middle of the screen was about dead center, and the red needle could go no higher.

It was quiet here. No traffic sped by, no pedestrians were abroad. The warrior slung the tracer over his left shoulder so both his hands would be free for combat. Most of the windows had curtains or draperies, which hindered him in viewing the occupants. In one house he did see an elderly matron washing dishes. In another a teenager watched television.

There were more than twenty homes between where Bolan stood and where the street curved around to an avenue. He couldn't very well go barging into each and every one. The residents would telephone the police, who might arrive before he found Dorsakov. They'd detain him, giving the rogue time to get away.

Bolan decided to take up a post at the middle of the row and keep watch on all the houses until his prey showed themselves. The river was lined with barges, a few with lights in their cabins, but he didn't give much thought to them until a door on one farther along opened and Roskov stepped into view.

The warrior crouched, his finger on the Uzi's trigger. Evidently Roskov hadn't seen him, as the former KGB agent walked to port and stared out over the Seine. A match flared in the darkness as a cigarette was lighted.

Bolan was sixty yards away, on the wrong side of the street. Keeping low, he crossed and made his way forward. He had covered twenty of the sixty yards when he heard a motor kick over. Straightening, the Executioner saw the barge being steered out into the river.

The big man sprinted toward the vessel. If he lost them now, it was all over. He fairly flew, but he reached the empty berth too late. The barge was fifty feet out and heading downriver. In time it would leave Paris behind. Eventually it would reach the English Channel. Dorsakov would make good his escape and hold another auction. And the next time he might carry it off.

Bolan kept on running, searching the shore for a small boat he could use. Well past the barges were several small piers where a score of craft were docked. He raced toward them, one eye on the barge, which cruised at a leisurely speed into the middle of the Seine. It was hundreds of yards away by the time he reached the piers. Other than an old man skinning a fish, they were deserted.

The warrior hardly hesitated. He dashed to a small motorboat, jumped in and cast off.

The old man looked up and called out as Bolan adjusted the throttle and gripped the starter rope. He pulled with all his might, yet all the motor did was sputter a few times. Again he pulled on the throttle. The fisherman had risen and was hurrying toward him, angrily shaking the skinning knife. Bolan wrenched on the rope once more. At last the motor caught, and without delay he guided the boat into the river in pursuit.

The barge was much bigger and heavier, but it also had a bigger motor and a substantial lead. For the next ten minutes Bolan had to content himself with merely keeping it in sight. Thankfully river traffic at that time of night was sparse. They went under a number of bridges and passed an island.

Bolan concentrated on narrowing the gap. It seemed as if he never would, then fate worked in his favor. The barge angled to the left bank and came to a stop at a wide landing.

The warrior slowed to a crawl and guided the motorboat close to the bank at a point several hundred feet from the barge. He could see figures moving about near the cabin but was unable to tell what they were up to. Letting the motor putter along, he looked for a place to land.

Just when Bolan saw a flat spot where the bank had been worn by erosion, the barge steered back out into the Seine again. The brief stop was difficult to explain but at least it had given him the chance to cut their lead by two-thirds. He revved the outboard and cruised toward the aft deck.

The barge moved at its top speed, as if Dorsakov were suddenly in a hurry to get somewhere. Bolan closed, yard by hard-earned yard. He saw cleats lining the deck and a reel of rope to starboard. The low, long cabin was situated in the center, its portholes ablaze with light.

Bolan drew within thirty feet, then twenty. He avoided the prop wash as best he was able, but it still buffeted the small craft, making it hard for him to steer straight. And his steering had to be precise if he was to accomplish the stunt he had in mind.

A cleat glistened dully at the starboard corner. Bolan maneuvered the motorboat steadily closer until its bow almost brushed the barge. He wedged the Uzi under his belt and slid the tracer under the seat. Standing, he gave himself a three-count, then went into action.

Bolan suddenly turned the steering arm at a sharp angle even as he killed the throttle and sprang onto the transom. For a frozen instant in time he was inches from the side of the barge. Muscles uncoiling, he leapt, his arms overhead, his fingers desperate to clutch the cleat that meant the difference between stopping Dorsakov and plunging into the Seine.

The warrior's left hand found purchase but his right missed. He smacked against the barge, the strain on his shoulder making him grit his teeth. Under him the motorboat veered off, its motor gradually dying until the craft was dead in the water but drifting toward the left bank, as he intended.

Spray moistened Bolan's face. He tried to raise his right arm high enough to grasp the cleat but couldn't quite reach it. Undaunted, he attempted to brace his shoes against the side but the smooth surface was too slick with moisture. His stomach tightened as he felt his left hand slipping.

And then Roskov appeared.

16

The Executioner held himself still as Roskov's dark silhouette blossomed at the side of the barge perhaps twenty feet distant. It was impossible for the Russian to have heard anything, yet he was gazing suspiciously out over the river. Roskov caught sight of the motorboat and moved toward the corner for a better look.

Bolan pressed his body close against the side. All the Russian had to do was look down and spot his hand, and it was all over. He reached for the Uzi and tried to pull it free, but it snagged on his belt and wouldn't budge. There was a cough above him. He could just distinguish the top of Roskov's head. Then the man grunted, spun on a heel and departed.

The warrior's left hand slipped a little more. He clamped his fingers tight, tucked his legs to his chest so his knees were against the barge and surged higher in a last-ditch attempt to snag the cleat. His right hand closed on the metal. Instantly he pulled himself up and over the side but froze short of the deck.

Roskov was only forty feet away, staring at something on the right bank.

Bolan hung from the cleat, as still as a rock. He saw the Russian move toward the cabin but stayed where he was in case the man unexpectedly turned. Almost too late he felt the Uzi sliding from under his belt. He grabbed it with his left hand, and was unable to hold himself off the deck. His shoulder hit with a soft thud.

The warrior glanced up, ready to fire even though it would forewarn Dorsakov. But Roskov never slowed. Moments later the cabin door framed him in a yellow glow, and he vanished within.

The Executioner sat up, rose into a crouch and crept along the gunwale. When he drew abreast of the first porthole, he ducked lower and scooted under it. Rising gingerly, he peeked inside, into an empty room. He moved around the cabin to the far side and went from porthole to porthole, looking for Mikhail Dorsakov and the Novichok-5.

He finally saw someone when halfway to the bow. Marya Dorsakov, her wrists and ankles tied, a gag over her mouth, lay on a berth. Her eyes were open, fixed on the ceiling.

Bolan went on. At the front of the cabin was the control room. It had been fitted with sophisticated consoles, the very latest in navigation gear, as if Dorsakov planned an open-sea voyage. Roskov was back at the controls. On a table against the opposite wall sat the metal case that contained the four vials.

As yet there had been no sign of Dorsakov, but Bolan wasn't about to let that stop him. Retrieving the Novichok-5 was his paramount priority. He stepped to the corner. A wide window afforded the pilot an unimpeded view of the river ahead, its bottom sill a good two feet off the deck. Lying on his belly, Bolan snaked the length of the window, rose and moved to a narrow door. Through a small porthole he saw Roskov examining a map on a console.

Bolan lightly placed his hand on the latch. He was all set to enter when he thought he heard a footstep aft.

Thinking it might be Dorsakov, and not caring to have the rogue come up behind him while he was busy with Roskov, he sank down and moved to intercept him.

The warrior traveled half the distance to the rear of the cabin but saw no one. He did come on another door, which he opened. A narrow companionway took him to a junction. Another led at right angles toward the control room. He reached the room where Kuragin was and slipped inside.

She turned. A strangled cry seeped through the gag. Swinging her legs over the side of the berth, she tried to sit up.

"Be still and be quiet," Bolan whispered, sinking to one knee. He removed the gag and threw it down. "I'll have you loose in a minute if you'll give me your word that you won't try to kill your father."

Kuragin had an air of panic about her. "He's not here!" she said. "He was put ashore awhile ago."

Bolan remembered the stop at the landing.

"Roskov is supposed to pick him up later downriver. But that's not important." She leaned down, her voice laced with terror. "You've got to stop him. He's going to use the Novichok-5."

"I saw the container in the control room."

"Only three vials are in it. He took one."

An icy chill rippled down the warrior's spine. "Did he say where he was going?"

"No. He went on and on about how he was going to teach our governments a lesson for hounding him, and how he would embarrass the agency. He claimed that by this time tomorrow, half the population of Paris would be dead."

Bolan turned her so he could untie her wrists. "How does he plan to unleash it? He can't just smash the vial on the ground and run. The agent spreads too fast. He'd be killed before he went ten feet."

Kuragin glanced over her shoulder. "I told him he was committing suicide, but he laughed and said that he had the perfect way worked out. All he needs is height and a strong wind. Those were his exact words."

"Height?" Bolan repeated thoughtfully, then paused as the rumble of the motor dropped in volume.

"We're slowing," Kuragin said. "But why so soon?"

"I have to find out," Bolan replied, giving one of the knots a final tug. "I'll be right back." He hurried to the door.

"Wait! Don't leave me like this!"

"I won't be long," Bolan assured her. As he raced toward the bow he wondered if the barge had a radio and if he would be able to get a call patched through to Brognola. The French authorities had to be warned so they could at least try to evacuate Paris before it was too late.

A closed door barred the warrior's path. Since time was of the essence, he lowered his shoulder and hit the thin wood panel with the force of a battering ram. The door buckled with a tremendous crash. Bolan stumbled but stayed on his feet and swung the Uzi toward the console where he had last seen Roskov. Only the Russian was gone.

The warrior glanced at the table and saw the metal case. Stepping to the wheel, he noticed the barge was making for the right bank. And the next moment his world exploded in pinwheels of light and waves of agony as a sledgehammer blow caught him between the shoulder blades, nearly snapping his spine. It drove him to his knees. The Uzi went skittering across the floor and smacked into the wall.

"Filthy American."

The words echoed through a haze of pain. Bolan shifted and saw Roskov rear above him. He swung at the Russian's legs, but the man was incredibly nimble for his size and bulk and danced aside. His arm was gripped in an iron vise. His feet left the floor, and he hit one of the consoles with enough force to break half the bones in his body. But he rolled on impact and kept himself loose. Springing to his feet unharmed, he whirled to face his enemy.

"I kill you with these," Roskov said, holding out his heavily callused hands.

Bolan stepped in close and flicked a two-punch combination that would have rocked most men on their heels. It was as if he'd struck a brick wall. Roskov merely grinned, seized Bolan by the front of the shirt and hurled him as if he were so much balsa wood.

This time Bolan's feet were swept out from under him, and he slid along the polished floor into the door to the outside. His head banged hard, and he lay stunned a few moments. When his vision cleared, he saw Roskov lumbering toward him like a grizzly. The Russian wore a sneer, confident in his strength and speed.

But the Executioner was far from finished. He waited until the absolute last moment and hurled himself at Roskov's ankles. The Russian jumped straight into the air to avoid being tripped, which suited Bolan almost as well, since all he had to do was grasp one of Roskov's ankles and heave. The Russian crashed down as Bolan scrambled up. He executed a spin kick, timed so that his heel caught Roskov in the face as the man rose. It bowled the Russian over, his nose broken.

Bolan closed, and barely evaded a slashing foot that would have shattered his kneecap. Circling, he feinted as his adversary jumped up, then delivered a blow to the ribs that made the Russian suck in his breath in torment. Before the Executioner could backpedal out of reach, Roskov thrust both hands around his throat and squeezed.

It was like being throttled by a short gorilla. Bolan punched his adversary's ribs but might as well have been striking a statue for all the effect it had. He spun, then twisted, trying to pry the man's thick fingers from his flesh. And when it became clear he couldn't, he kicked the Russian in the groin.

Roskov vented a strangled gasp, his grip slackening. Bolan drove both his arms up and in. His wrists smashed his enemy's brawny arms aside, allowing him to pivot, cock an elbow and spear a sword-hand thrust into the base of the Russian's throat.

Roskov staggered and inhaled raggedly but wouldn't go down. He lunged, clawing for the warrior's eyes.

Bolan ducked under the raking nails, gripped one of Roskov's wrists, spun and flipped the man over his shoulder. The Russian slammed into the wall, cracking the panel. He landed on his side, battered and wheezing but not out of the fight yet. His hand plunged under his jacket.

The warrior saw the Uzi lying on the floor nearby. He leapt for the subgun as Roskov's Walther appeared, the crack of the shot loud in the confined control room. At such close range under normal circumstances the Russian would never have missed, but the beating he had taken made it hard for him to hold his arm steady. The slug struck the window, lacing it with spiderwebs. A second shot rang out as Bolan scooped the Uzi into his hands. Extending the weapon, he fired a burst into Roskov's face.

Wearily Bolan stood. He went to claim the Walther, then recalled with a start that the barge had been heading toward the right bank. He whirled and discovered the bow was too close to a dock to avert a collision. Throwing himself at the wheel, he hung on, his legs braced.

A splintering crash rent the night. The jolt nearly knocked Bolan to the floor but he was able to hold on and stay upright. When the vessel steadied itself, he looked out.

The bow had sheared through the dock as if it were so much kindling, and run aground. It was sheer luck no one had been in front of it and been crushed to a pulp.

Bolan picked up the Walther, grabbed the metal case and hurried back down the companionway. "Marya," he called as he neared her door. "We have to hurry." He burst inside, then stopped in his tracks. The berth was empty, the ropes that had bound her were lying on the floor.

The Executioner turned and hurried out of the cabin, heading aft. At the gunwale he scanned the surface and spotted her, swimming smoothly, hundreds of feet away. "Marya!" he shouted.

She slowed, glanced back for a few moments, then resumed stroking.

Bolan was puzzled. Why was she risking a swim to the far shore when it made more sense for the two of them to join forces to hunt down her father? Or had she lied to him about knowing where Dorsakov went? He idly lifted his gaze to the Paris skyline, and suddenly he saw the answer to both questions, right there in front of his eyes. It was so obvious he should have realized it sooner.

Sirens wailed, a familiar sound to Bolan by now. People were converging on the shattered dock. Soon some of them would venture on board.

The warrior sprinted back into the cabin. He took a long piece of rope from the room where Kuragin had been, then returned aft. Verifying the latches to the case were closed securely, he looped the rope around the handle several times and around the case itself several more. Next he made a large loop, tied four knots so the rope would never come undone, then shrugged into the loop, angling it across his chest.

Prepared, Bolan went over the side. He hung from the gunwale and dropped cleanly into the water in order not to jar the vials. As he faced the far bank, he saw Kuragin clambering out. She staggered, on the verge of exhaustion. Seconds later the darkness swallowed her up.

Bolan hurried as fast as he thought it safe to go. He knew the vials were cushioned by thick padding inside and protected by the unbreakable metal outside, but that hardly seemed protection enough given the deadliness of the Novichok-5. He reached the halfway point and stopped to look back.

Patrol cars had arrived at the scene. Their flashing lights revealed scores of bystanders. Policemen were on the barge, some with flashlights.

A beam speared out over the Seine, then another. Bolan saw one sweep toward him. He gulped in air and dived, paddling slowly. When his lungs were almost oxygen starved, he surfaced. The police still searched the river, forcing him to dive again. The cold water chilled his skin, and his clothes clung to him like limp weights. Given all he had been through, it was a marvel of stamina that he was able to keep on going.

Bolan's limbs were leaden when he finally crawled out of the Seine and lurched to his feet. He should have found a telephone to contact Brognola, but he had no time to spare. Willing his legs to move, he jogged to a street, then headed to a major artery. Not one taxi appeared, and he was still at least two miles from the landmark.

Then the warrior spotted a young man unlocking the door to a parked car. He ran over and leaned on the hood, almost out of breath. The young man looked up, startled.

"Don't be afraid," Bolan said. "Please. I need your help. I must get to the Eiffel Tower quickly!" He shoved a hand in his pocket for the wad of francs Brognola had given him. "I'll pay you," he added, waving the money. The man studied him. Bolan was ready to wrestle the keys loose, if need be, and take the car by force. He walked around the fender, the francs in front of him.

"Are you hurt?" the man asked.

"No."

"Why are you wet? And what is that on your back?"

"I have no time to explain." Bolan reached the front door. "Will you take me or not? It's a matter of life and death."

"I suppose I am crazy, but *oui,* I will. Get in."

Bolan adjusted the case so it was under his left arm. Then, before the man could react, he tore the keys from the owner's hand, threw open the door and slid behind the wheel. "Hurry up," he urged.

The young man's mouth dropped. "Wait a minute, *monsieur!* I thought you meant for me to drive. I let no one drive my car, ever."

Bolan glanced at him. "You have two choices. You can stand here and watch your precious car drive off, or you can get in the passenger side and go for the ride of your life."

"I—I—I—" the Frenchman sputtered, not quite knowing what to say. He gasped as the big man started his car, then darted around to the other side and climbed in.

The instant the young man's backside touched the seat, Bolan shifted and peeled out, veering into the traffic flow without regard for oncoming traffic. Horns blared. Drivers cursed eloquently in French.

The owner appeared about to be ill. *"Mon Dieu!"* he cried. "Please be careful!"

Bolan gained the passing lane and shot toward the Eiffel Tower. It was an impressive structure—seven thousand tons of iron and steel held together by almost three million rivets. It soared nine hundred and eighty-four feet into the air, and for many years had been the highest structure in the world. Kuragin's words came back to him. "All he needs is height and a strong wind." Nowhere else in Paris would Mikhail Dorsakov find the two so perfectly combined. If Dorsakov unleashed the Novichok-5 from the tower's peak, Paris was doomed.

The traffic was heavy. Bolan leaned on the horn to get a slowpoke out of his path. When the other driver refused to give, he swung into the middle lane and shot past.

"You must have a death wish!" the owner wailed.

Bolan glanced at him. "Do you know what a biochemical weapon is?"

"A what?" the man said, bewildered. "Why, yes, as a matter of fact, I do. My English is quite good, is it not? I studied it in secondary school as do most—"

"I don't have time to hear about your bubblegum days," Bolan interrupted. "Just pay attention. When I get out, go find the police." He paused. It would have been so much easier if the press had gotten wind of Dorsakov's theft and reported the story worldwide. But the Russian government had clamped a tight lid on the case. And other governments had followed their example. None was eager to let its citizenry know a madman was on the loose armed with the most lethal biochemical agent ever created.

"A man is planning to unleash a biochemical weapon from the Eiffel Tower," Bolan revealed. "You have to let the police know. Tell them to contact La Sûreté Nationale if they won't believe you."

The owner laughed nervously. "Oh, please. You expect me to accept such a—how would you say—tall tale? Seriously you must have drunk too much wine, *monsieur.*"

Bolan grabbed the man by the arm and pulled him closer. "Do you smell any alcohol on my breath?" he growled.

"No," the owner said, abruptly scared.

"Do I look like I'm playing some sort of game?"

"No. Not at all."

"Then do as I tell you. If you want, put a phone call to La Sûreté Nationale direct. They'll believe you."

"Can it be?" the man said, horrified, and gazed through the windshield, dumbfounded. "But why would anyone do such a thing?"

Bolan had no time or inclination to lecture the man on the nature of evil. He focused on his driving and pushed the car to its limit. When, eventually, he screeched to a stop in front of the monument, he found the area packed with sightseers, skateboarders and citizens out for a stroll. "Do as I told you," he reminded the owner, then turned and jogged toward the base of the edifice.

As Bolan recalled, the Eiffel Tower had four platforms, or levels. A restaurant was on the bottom one, while the second and third platforms were bars. All three would be crowded, hardly ideal spots for Dorsakov to rig the vial. No, Bolan knew the Russian would go all the way to the top. There was a television transmitter up there, a meteorological station, and, best of all from Dorsakov's point of view, an observation platform.

The warrior swung the metal case behind his back and tightened the rope. He ran up the stairs to the lower level, then over to the elevators where he impatiently waited for one to descend. Every second was vital. He could feel it in his bones. Some of the other waiting people gave him curious glances, but he ignored them.

When the elevator finally arrived, Bolan was the first one in. He couldn't allow the others to board, so he blocked the doorway and motioned them back. Most were too flabbergasted to argue. A few started forward, and he had to shove a burly man who tried to squeeze past. The door closed before any of them could make an issue of it, and their angry shouts rose in the air with the car.

Bolan stabbed the button for the observation platform. Now that he was close to his goal, he had a new problem to solve, namely how to stop Dorsakov when he had no weapon. He stared out over the city's myriad twinkling lights, estimating how far he had climbed and how far he had to go. The elevator passed the second platform, then the third.

When the car came to a stop, the warrior pressed against the side. He didn't want Dorsakov to spot him right away—if, indeed, the rogue was still there. For all Bolan knew, Dorsakov had already planted the vial and gone.

There were four sides to the observation deck, thanks to a square platform that enclosed the central core housing the elevator shafts. About a dozen tourists filled the narrow space in front of the car. Bolan eased out and sidled to the left, his back to the elevator. He came to the first corner. Neither Dorsakov nor Kuragin were anywhere to be seen, so he went on.

Suddenly a score of men, women and children came rushing around the next corner, all in a panic, all talking at once. Bolan tried to make sense of their jumbled statements but caught only a few words, among them, loud and clear, "gun." He jogged to the corner. The east section of the platform was deserted. Then he heard voices and looked up.

A metal ladder rose from the observation deck to a smaller platform that housed the meteorological station and the television transmitters. Mikhail Dorsakov stood at one end, a pistol in one hand, the vial of Novichok-5 in the other. His daughter was at the top of the ladder, coaxing him softly in Russian, trying to get him to lower the vial, to give it to her.

Dorsakov kept refusing. He took a step toward her, the vial poised overhead. Then he glanced down and spotted the Executioner. "Well, well, well. If it isn't our American friend."

Kuragin twisted and gestured at Bolan. "Get out of here. Leave this to me."

"No way."

"You both must go!" Dorsakov demanded, staring at his daughter. "Please, Marya. I've no desire to harm you. But I will not be denied, not at this stage."

The warrior edged nearer to the ladder while undoing the knots so he could lower the case to the floor. From far below wafted the blare of car horns, the growl of traffic, and, ever so faintly, laughter and voices, the sounds of life that would be extinguished forever if that vial fell.

"Your concern, Father, is touching," Kuragin said scornfully. "Where was it when I was a child? Why did you neglect me all those years if you really cared?" She moved a little closer to him, her arms at her sides.

Bolan had all the knots undone except one. He pried and pried, but it refused to budge.

"This is not the time or place to justify myself to you," Dorsakov said. "Come with me and I will tell you everything. And after I sell the remaining vials, I will share my wealth with you. We will forget all about the old days and start our lives over."

"You're deluding yourself, Father. There is no turning back, not after what you have done. Not for you or for me. The agency will see to that."

"I spit on them," Dorsakov said, and spit over the side.

Unnoticed by either of them, Bolan had removed the container and set it next to the metal ladder. He put a foot on the lower rung and reached for a higher one.

"How ironic that you should hate them so," Kuragin stated, "because that is exactly how I feel about you."

Bolan saw it coming before Dorsakov. "Marya, don't!" he yelled, but it was too late. She hurled herself at her father. Her fingers closed on his wrists, and she batted his gun hand against the rail in an effort to shake the pistol loose. Dorsakov seemed shocked by her attack and for a few moments failed to resist. Then he kneed her in the thigh, causing her right leg to buckle. Desperately she hung on, pulling him down with her.

The Executioner flew to her aid. He fixed his gaze on the vial, which waved wildly as Dorsakov struggled. Twice it came close to being smashed against the Tower. Bolan was only one rung below the platform when Kuragin suddenly surged upward, hooked a foot behind her father's leg and tried to trip him. Instead, she sent Dorsakov toppling over the low rail, and she fell with him.

The warrior swung to the left and lunged at the vial, trying to snag it. He just missed. They dropped past him, twisting in midair as they struggled. Bolan was sure the vial would shatter when they hit, but Kuragin wound up on the bottom and bore the brunt of the impact, cushioning her father, who held the vial high so it wouldn't break. She was dazed, and made no move to stop Dorsakov as he rose unsteadily and backed toward the rail.

Bolan had been a bystander long enough. He launched himself from the ladder and landed right next to Dorsakov. The renegade tried to leap back, but the warrior caught both his wrists, as Kuragin had done, and wrenched on the left one. The Makarov clattered at their feet, allowing Bolan to devote all his attention to the vial.

Mikhail Dorsakov was furious. "Damn you, American!" he snarled, and tried to knee the warrior as he had his daughter.

Bolan evaded the blow with a jerk of his hips. He knew that all the Russian had to do was let go of the vial and they were all dead, so he shifted his grip, clamping his hand over Dorsakov's so the man couldn't open his fingers. At the same time he used an ankle sweep and slammed the Russian onto his back.

The warrior got a knee on Dorsakov's left arm, pinning it. He had to pry the vial loose before it was too late. But Dorsakov fought like a madman, wrenching his right arm free and flailing, battering Bolan's chest and face. The Executioner blocked as many blows as he could while working on Dorsakov's left hand.

A crazed gleam had come into the Russian's eyes. He heaved, his spine arching, and succeeded in throwing Bolan off him. The warrior was able to keep his grip on his adversary's left hand, but that was all. Dorsakov pushed to his feet, as did Bolan. For a moment they were face-to-face, the Russian panting, the warrior as grim as death.

"You will not stop me, American. If I must, I will take you with me."

Bolan's response was to kick the ex-spy in the shin. Dorsakov buckled, and as he did, Bolan tucked his hip against the other man's and executed a hip toss that smashed Dorsakov down at his feet. The warrior drove both knees into the Russian's stomach. Dorsakov weakened, and Bolan, seeing his chance, tried to wrest the vial loose.

Dorsakov still had fight left, though. He also had the Makarov.

Out of the corner of an eye Bolan saw the 9 mm pistol rising toward his ribs. He swung an elbow, deflecting the barrel just as the pistol discharged. The slug ricocheted off the Eiffel Tower. Dorsakov, growling in his chest like an animal, pounded the gun against Bolan's arm, numbing it from the shoulder to the wrist.

The Executioner tried to grab the gun, but his arm refused to cooperate.

Dorsakov laughed.

The warrior didn't dare let go of the hand holding the vial. He was at the Russian's mercy, and Dorsakov knew it.

Wearing a superior smirk, the rogue raised the Makarov a second time and took aim. Kuragin came hurtling at them from out of nowhere. She got both of her hands on her father's wrist and tried to shake the pistol loose. Dorsakov resisted, swinging his arm as if it were a club in an attempt to dislodge her. Without either of them being aware of it, the muzzle nuzzled her stomach, and then there was a shot. For a few moments no one moved.

Kuragin slowly stiffened, her cheeks going white as a red stain blossomed on her blouse. She released her father and stepped back, confusion and hurt on her face. "How—" she said weakly.

"No!" Dorsakov shouted as his daughter's features went slack and she melted to the floor. He stared at her a second, then went berserk.

It was all Bolan could do to keep his grip on Dorsakov's right hand. The renegade hit and kicked him in a frenzy, determined to hurl the vial at all costs, no longer caring if he lived or died. They grappled, rolling back and forth across the floor.

Bolan winced as he was rammed into the rail. He managed to rise on one knee and was punched in the stomach. With both his hands covering the vial so it wouldn't fall, he had to resist with his knees and feet, which he did by tramping down hard on the Russian's instep and then driving his knee into Dorsakov's face.

The warrior felt the rogue sag. Quickly he inserted several fingers under Dorsakov's and peeled them loose enough to partially grip the vial. Before he could palm it, the Russian flared to life and clipped him on the temple. Bolan shrugged off the blow and wriggled his fingers farther around the vial.

"You cannot win!" Dorsakov raged.

Bolan suddenly realized the Russian was trying to crush the vial. He resisted, his shoulder and arm muscles rippling, his hand shaking from the terrific strain. Dorsakov hissed, rose to his knees and resorted to the gambit of last resort—he tried to bite Bolan's neck.

The warrior yanked his head back out of reach, then reversed himself, ramming his forehead into the renegade's face. Not once, but three times, so hard it hurt his own neck. Dorsakov drooped, nearly senseless, his fingers loosening. In one swift motion Bolan tore the vial from the Russian's grasp, rose and stepped back. Dorsakov went after him. Bolan dodged a frantic rush, then delivered a snap kick to the Russian's chest that sent him sailing up and over the top rail.

Mikhail Dorsakov screamed as he fell, a scream that went on and on, wavering on the wind every inch of the thousand-foot drop.

The Executioner turned as the scream abruptly choked off. He opened the metal case and carefully placed the fourth vial back where it belonged. Then, just as carefully, he closed the case and latched it. The threat was ended. For a while, at least, the world was safe.

Blazing a perilous trail through
the heart of darkness

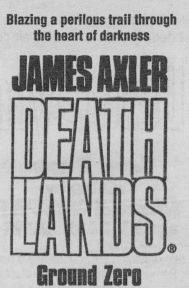

JAMES AXLER
DEATH LANDS®

Ground Zero

Ryan Cawdor and his band of survivalists search for a better future
in the devastated ruins of a city once called Washington. Facing
double jeopardy posed by a barbaric baron, and the indifferent
wrath of nature, Ryan Cawdor and his band of warrior survivalists
are determined to persevere against predatory foes.

In the Deathlands, everyone and everything is fair game, but only
the strongest survive.

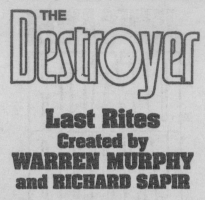